STAR TREK™ EXPLORER

THE OFFICIAL MAGAZINE

PRESENTS

"Q AND FALSE" AND OTHER STORIES

STAR TREK™ EXPLORER

THE OFFICIAL MAGAZINE

PRESENTS

"Q AND FALSE" AND OTHER STORIES

The short stories contained in the book feature characters and situations from acoss the *Star Trek* universe, including *Star Trek Enterprise, Star Trek, Star Trek: The Next Generation, Star Trek: Deep Space Nine,* and *Star Trek: Voyager.*

These mini-epics, written by acclaimed *Star Trek* authors, include the strange tale of James T. Kirk's encounter with the mysterious, seemingly omnipotent being, known as Q, get swept up in an adventure with the dashing Captain Proton, and join Doctor Beverly Crusher as she battles to save Worf from some ferocious predators.

EDITORIAL
Editor: Jonathan Wilkins
Designer: Dan Bura
Group Editor: Jake Devine
Editorial Assistant: Calum Collins
Copy Editor: Phoebe Hedges
Art Director: Oz Browne
Production Controllers: Caterina Falqui & Kelly Fenlon
Production Manager: Jackie Flook
Marketing Coordinator: Lauren Noding
Publicity Manager: Will O'Mullane
Publicity & Sales Coordinator: Alexandra Iciek
Sales & Circulation Manager: Steve Tothill

Digital & Marketing Manager: Jo Teather
Acquisitions Editor: Duncan Baizley
Publishing Directors: Ricky Claydon & John Dziewiatkowski
Group Operations Director: Alex Ruthen
Executive Vice President: Andrew Sumner
Publishers: Vivian Cheung & Nick Landau

DISTRIBUTION
U.S. Distribution: Penguin Random House
U.K. Distribution: MacMillan Distribution
Direct Sales Market: Diamond Comic Distributors
General Inquiries: customerservice@titanpublishingusa.com

Star Trek Explorer Presents "Q and False" and Other Stories
ISBN: 978-1787738621
Published by Titan
A division of Titan Publishing Group Ltd., 144 Southwark Street, London SE1 0UP, TM ® & © 2022 CBS Studios Inc. © 2022 Paramount Pictures. STAR TREK and Related Marks are Trademarks of CBS Studios Inc. All Rights Reserved. Titan Authorised User. CBS, the CBS Eye logo and related marks are trademarks of CBS Broadcasting Inc. TM & © 2022 CBS Broadcasting Inc. All rights reserved.

A CIP catalogue record for this title is available from the British Library.
First Edition December 2022
10 9 8 7 6 5 4 3 2 1
Printed in China.

Paramount Global: Marian Cordry
Copyright Promotions Ltd.: Anna Hatjoullis
Paramount Home Entertainment: Kate Addy, Jiella Esmat, Liz Hadley, and John Robson
Simon & Schuster US: Ed Schlesinger

Contents

A *STAR TREK* STORY

All That Most Maddens and Torments

STORY: CHRISTOPHER COOPER
ILLUSTRATION: KLEBS JR

sudden torrent of icy black water slammed across the deck, tearing the helmsman from the wheel and whipping him away into the boiling darkness, his petrified screams lost in the howling wind.

Captain James T. Kirk lunged forward and grabbed at the helm, its spokes spinning furiously. Gripping the handles, he clung to the wheel and set his whole weight against it, struggling to keep his vessel on course as his ship bucked and lurched ferociously towards starboard. He knew his crew, too, would be playing their part, doing all that they could to guide her safely through this maelstrom. Another wave hit, threatening to loosen Kirk's grip on the heavy wooden wheel and drag him tumbling overboard. Somehow, the captain held firm and redoubled his efforts, his mouth clenched tightly shut as salt water forced its way through his nostrils.

Then, just as quickly as it had begun, the violence of the storm had passed, leaving Kirk exhausted and bewildered, his ship adrift on a suddenly calm sea. He watched the tumult of clouds drifting away, orange and electric blue sparks skipping unnaturally between them, the spectacle dissipating as it drifted towards the horizon, leaving only stars sparkling in the cool night sky.

Kirk felt out of place, out of time. Where was he?

"Fascinating."

For the briefest of moments, Kirk's heart lifted. Spock! But how could it be? His old friend was so very far away. He didn't care to recall how long it had been since they'd last spoken.

"Captain, are you injured?" The voice spoke again. No, not Spock. Someone else. A voice that was warm, measured, with a hint of concern, yet also… mischief?

Standing close by was a tall, debonair individual whom Kirk didn't recognize as a member of his crew and knew instinctively was not a man to be trusted. The ostentatious admiral's uniform he was wearing was also something of a giveaway.

"Who are you, and what are you doing on my ship?" Kirk demanded.

"Now, now, mon Capitan. Is that any way to welcome a superior officer?" The Admiral smirked.

"They'll promote anyone these days," Kirk replied, as he quickly took the measure of the man. He had a classically noble face, with features worthy of a Michelangelo sculpture and fathomless eyes that overflowed with self-importance, as if he knew all the secrets of creation but preferred to keep them under his bicorne hat.

"Your name, 'Admiral.'" Kirk insisted. "Or perhaps you'd like to take a tour of my ship, starting with the brig?"

"Admiral Q at your disposal," replied Q with a respectful bow. "It is my honor to finally make your acquaintance, Captain James Tiberius Kirk. I've heard so much about you."

"Admiral… 'Q?'"

"Mon plaisir."

"Never heard of you."

"I precede my reputation."

"That's probably for the best. The brig is this way."

"I'm sure your facilities are most comfortable, but there'll be time for that soon enough. I would say you have a more pressing concern," said Q, glancing out to sea.

Kirk frowned and turned to peer in the direction the stranger had indicated. He saw nothing at first, then a snow-white dorsal fin broke the still surface, perhaps 200 yards to port, followed by a broad, glistening back, riven by ugly scars.

"There she blows," came a cry from somewhere ahead.

"Is that… a whale?" Kirk murmured to himself, observing the majestic sight. Why did he feel such a pressing compulsion to pursue it?

"Astonishing creatures," marveled Q. "And most excellent company. How they tolerated humankind for so long, I'll never understand. I believe you have some history there?"

Kirk continued to stare after the whale, lost in a memory he couldn't quite connect with. "Yes. Yes, I suppose I do," he said distantly.

"Then you must act with the utmost alacrity, otherwise the leviathan will defy you once again," Q declared, but Kirk barely heard him above the sudden pounding of blood in his ears. There was no time to waste.

"Hoist the mainsail. Ahead, maximum speed!" he bellowed, once again taking the helm, thoughts of the intruder slipping from his mind. All he knew was that he had to catch that whale, at any cost.

The ship tacked towards the beast and began to gain speed. A strong following wind had whipped up as if in answer to Kirk's direct order, and the ship's vast canvas sails billowed majestically, carrying the vessel closer, ever closer, to its prey. Kirk grinned, enjoying the rush of clean, unfiltered air and sea spray against his skin. This must have been how it felt to command such a glorious craft all those centuries ago… and Kirk caught himself mid-thought.

He wasn't where he should be. None of this made sense.

"Don't lose focus, dear Captain," Q reassured him, his eyes sparkling with rapt interest. "You have a mission to complete."

Kirk blinked. He could feel the contours of the wheel's handles, the sodden cloth against his skin, smell the salt air… "But this isn't real. None of it. This can't be possible!" he told himself, struggling to reconcile his sense of self with the world happening around him.

"What is reality but a construct of your own mind?" said Q. "What you perceive is all that matters."

Kirk gazed at the stranger, who now stood at the captain's shoulder with a look of glee on his face. There was something about this 'Q' that seemed familiar, but Kirk couldn't quite place it. For no reason, a giant black cat sprang into his thoughts. "Did you create all this?" Kirk heard

himself ask, although he didn't know quite why.

"I am merely a casual observer," Q smiled back. "But believe me, I am thrilled to be here, for this moment."

The sound of raised voices on the main deck caught Kirk's attention. Several men were preparing a device of some kind, a contraption of brass and polished wood, mounted on a pivot at the prow of the ship. He watched as they loaded it with gunpowder and slipped a steel rod with a barbed spike at the end into the barrel. Kirk felt his blood run cold. A harpoon gun. This ship – his ship – was a whaler!

"No," he gasped. How could he ever be party to such slaughter? Whatever it was he was experiencing, the disconnect to any recognizable reality hit Kirk like a hammer. Was his mind no longer his own? Was some external force weighing down on the instincts he had always relied on? Fighting against the fug of paranoia, Kirk knew one thing – Q was at the center of all this.

"What are you doing to me?" Kirk challenged his tormentor, their faces mere inches apart. What he didn't expect to find was sorrow and respect in the man's eyes.

"This is all you," Q answered, gently.

"Then why would I invite you along for the ride? What are you, Q?"

"A long-time admirer, making up for missed opportunities," said Q, quite sincerely. "Opportunities which you are running out of."

Kirk frowned. "Is that a threat?"

"An observation," replied Q.

A sudden cry from the rigging interrupted Kirk's thoughts. "Ship ahoy!"

He hurried over to the port bulwark and scanned the sea. There, closing in fast and evidently with the same target in its sights was another whaler, her hull adorned with row upon row of ivory teeth, daggers ripped from the jaws of its conquests and set in a grimace that lent the vessel the look of a vile, skeletal predator. The captain stared at the aged ship in disbelief. It surely hailed straight from the pages of a novel he'd first read as a schoolboy.

"It's the *Pequod*!"

Q's eyes widened; a look of genuine shock flashed across his face. "Did you say… Picard?!"

"*Pequod*," Kirk corrected him. He felt like laughing. "The *Pequod*. From the novel, *Moby Dick*. Captain Ahab's ship." Despite everything his senses were telling him, Kirk was now in no doubt that this world, all of it, was a work of fiction. Q's fiction.

"I admit, I'm not much of a reader," Q blustered, and Kirk could have sworn that for some reason he looked relieved. Determined to rectify that, he grabbed the fake admiral by the collar.

"You're going to tell me where you've taken me, right now," Kirk demanded.

"Don't disappoint me, Captain. You're so much better than some muscle-headed thug. I expect more of you."

"What is this place? Where am I? Tell me!"

"Priorities, mon Capitan. I am not your enemy."

Kirk suddenly remembered the creature he was pursuing, the grim silhouette of the *Pequod* bearing down on it, and the loaded harpoon gun on his own ship. Real or not, the fate of the great white whale rested in his hands.

The *Pequod* was now alongside, racing past Kirk's ship, and he could hear its captain screaming orders at the

> KIRK GAZED AT THE STRANGER, WHO NOW STOOD AT THE CAPTAIN'S SHOULDER WITH A LOOK OF GLEE ON HIS FACE. THERE WAS SOMETHING ABOUT THIS 'Q' THAT SEEMED FAMILIAR…

crew – deranged, determined, just as he'd always imagined Ahab's voice to sound. He looked across to see if he could get a glimpse of the infamous literary figure but was surprised when he finally located him. Ahab was nothing like the bearded whaler described in the book. This man was dressed more like a pirate, grey hair falling across tanned skin, a battered pendant shining against his bare, muscular chest. Kirk recognized that insignia. It was part of him. Part of who he was. And he knew the man, too.

"Khan," Q observed. "Fascinating."

Releasing Q, Kirk vaulted over the balustrade that separated the helm from the main deck and hurtled towards the men who were already aiming their harpoon gun at the beleaguered white whale. A few of them put up a fight, but Kirk soon wrested control of the weapon from them.

"You have a choice to make, Captain Kirk," Q shouted, somehow still at Kirk's side. "Vengeance or victory. Which will it be?"

"If you think those are my only options, you don't know me at all," Kirk shouted back.

He swung the harpoon gun away from the whale and for a moment Khan was centered in its crosshairs. But killing Khan was not Kirk's intent. Finding his target, he fired. In a flash of gunpowder, the harpoon lashed out, trailing strong rope behind it, and found its mark. With a thundering impact, the barbed arrowhead buried itself deep into the uppermost third of the *Pequod*'s rudder.

"Hard to starboard," Kirk bellowed.

He felt his ship turn instantly and watched the harpoon line pull taught. Then came the roar of straining, splintering wood, and the *Pequod*'s rudder tore away from its fixings, taking a good section of hull along with it. Kirk barely registered Khan's angry reaction, more concerned with the glistening shape in the water now making good on its chance for freedom. He watched as Moby Dick swam away, white skin bathed in starlight, and was reminded of a ship named *Enterprise*.

* * *

Kirk blinked. Sulu and Chekov were calmly monitoring the ship's navigation systems. Commander Scott was helping Uhura configure her communications station, and Spock was discussing sensor readings with Bones. He was back on his ship. On the *Enterprise*. But…

"Well done, Captain. I knew you had it in you," said Q, delighted.

Kirk rose from his chair and stepped towards the maddening visitor, his memories falling back into place. "What is this all about, Q? Why am I here, of all places?"

"The bridge of the *U.S.S. Enterprise*, NCC-1701. The place you were happiest of all," Q smiled, still wearing his admiral's outfit. "You made it. You should be proud of yourself."

"This ship was retired long ago," Kirk said, although how he longed for that not to be so. "I was on the *Enterprise*-B. She was caught in a gravimetric distortion. Was that your doing?"

"A little. The result of youthful exuberance for which I can only apologize," Q shrugged. "But you're missing the point. You've survived the trauma, held on to the essence of 'you'. Not everyone who transitions into the Nexus is so fortunate. I'm impressed."

"The 'Nexus'?"

"I've said too much already, and I really shouldn't be here," Q waved, dismissively. "You'll get used to the place soon enough. Farewell, mon Capitan. It has been my honor."

And Q remained exactly where he was standing, confusion etched on his brow. "Now, this is unexpected," he murmured, distractedly. "Why am I still wearing this ridiculous uniform?"

Kirk considered Q for a moment and understood. "'This is all you.' That's what you said."

"Did I?" Q looked evasive.

"Moby Dick, the *Pequod*… I conjured them from my mind. My memories."

"You did."

"And this too. This *Enterprise*," Kirk looked around his bridge, recalling how much he'd loved his ship, his crew. "I control this reality."

Q remained silent.

"Which means you can't go anywhere without my say-so," Kirk reasoned.

"Would you really wish to spend an eternity in here, with me?"

Kirk considered this. "Fair point," he said. "But I have to know. The ship – out of danger?"

"Yes," said Q. "Now, if you'd excuse me, I have other captains to entertain."

Less than an instant later, Q was gone. ⭐

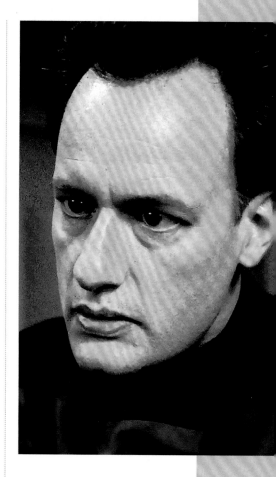

■ **A former editor of *Star Trek Magazine*, Christopher Cooper is a novelist, comic strip writer, cartoonist, and playwright. His full-cast audio drama, *Torchwood: Sargasso*, was a finalist in the 2020 Scribe Awards, and his latest *Doctor Who* audio drama is available now.**

■ **Klebs Jr is a Brazilian artist and writer who runs IHQ Studios. His work has appeared in titles by DC, Marvel, Malibu, Valiant and more. He recently published his graphic novel, *Country at Arms*, which won the HQMIX award in Brazil for best mini-series.**

A *STAR TREK THE NEXT GENERATION* STORY

Q and False

STORY: LISA KLINK
ILLUSTRATION: CHRISTIAN ROSADO

aptain Jean-Luc Picard was sweating under the trinary suns of Nvarat Prime. His dress uniform felt like it was suffocating him. Whose idea had it been to have this reception outdoors? He had to admit that the clusters of pale blue trees swaying in the light breeze were beautiful, especially set against the elegantly curved Nvarati architecture. He took a cold glass of what was supposed to be lemonade from a nearby table. Their hosts had gone to considerable trouble to provide food and drink that would please their guests. The Nvarati wanted to make a good impression on the visiting members of the *Enterprise* crew, consisting of Picard, Lieutenant Worf, and Counselor Deanna Troi, who were here to determine whether or not to recommend the Nvarati for membership in the Federation. So far, Picard was inclined to give them his approval.

Troi approached him. Picard noticed that she was sweating, too. "First Minister Hrakon certainly has a high opinion of himself."

"Yes, I noticed that." He glanced over at Worf, who was currently talking with the First Minister. Or, more accurately, listening to the man expound on the virtues of Nvaratan society as he gestured emphatically with all four of his arms. The Nvarati were shorter than the average human and covered in long white fur, which they adorned with beads and jewels as a mark of status.

"He has every reason to be proud of everything his people have achieved," said Picard. "Did you see their quantum flux generators? Extraordinary."

"True. But I'd be more interested to find out if they've discovered air-conditioning."

Picard smiled in the stifling heat. "Perhaps it's time to request a tour of the interior of these lovely buildings."

They heard some raised voices on the other side of the paved patio. A Nvarati woman emerged from the surrounding jungle and collapsed into the arms of two reception guests.

"Help me…" she said weakly.

"Water!" called one of the others.

Picard, Worf, and Troi joined the group who gathered around the newcomer. Someone brought over a translucent container of fresh water and gave it to the woman, who drank gratefully. Her white fur was matted with dirt and she was dressed very differently from the sleek, spotlessly clean diplomats attending the reception, in rough fabric that hung from her gaunt frame.

"Are you injured?" asked Worf.

She shook her head and took another long drink of water. Troi knelt down next to her. "I'm Deanna. What's your name?"

"Masang."

The First Minister pushed to the front of the group. He looked the woman up and down with a disgusted expression. "Oh. She's one of *them*."

"Not anymore," Masang insisted. "I escaped from the Sliani. They were going to kill me, as a sacrifice to the All Powerful."

Second Minister Petrallin turned to Picard. "The Sliani are a religious cult. They have some… unusual practices." The Nvarati hosting the *Enterprise* delegation were an atheistic society, which seemed to be a particular source of pride for Hrakon.

"Including human sacrifice?" asked Picard.

"No," Masang protested. "Never before. But our livestock have been dying this year. And the new Grand Talik says that a blood offering is necessary to appease the All Powerful."

Hrakon scoffed. "Insanity."

The Sliani woman turned to him. "I want to request sanctuary."

Everyone stared at the First Minister, waiting for his answer. He glanced over at Picard, then said, "Yes. Of course." He gestured to one of his aides. "Take her to the medical complex to get checked out. And get her something to eat."

Masang went to the Prime Minister and pressed the palms of her hands against his. "Thank you." Then the aide led her away.

Hrakon turned back to his guests. "We'll take good care of her. Now, who would like a tour of the cultural center?"

Picard wasn't so easily distracted. "Your application to the Federation didn't mention any other cultural groups on this world."

"The Sliani are such a small minority, it hardly seemed significant." He displayed the Nvarati version of a smile, which looked more like a human yawn.

"We consider the treatment of minorities to be very significant," said Picard.

Worf faced the Prime Minister. "We need to meet with these Sliani before we can make a decision."

The man stammered, trying to come up with a suitable response, when Petrallin stepped forward. "Yes. I'm sorry we didn't think to arrange that."

Hrakon glared at his Second Minister. "Unfortunately, they have no communications technology. We'll have to send a messenger to the nearest settlement…"

"Or someone can escort us there," Troi suggested.

"I'll take them," Petrallin offered.

"Thank you," said Picard.

The Second Minister led them to a Nvarati hovercraft, barely large

> A NVARATI WOMAN EMERGED FROM THE SURROUNDING JUNGLE AND COLLAPSED INTO THE ARMS OF TWO RECEPTION GUESTS.

enough for himself and the three Federation delegates. They left the capital city and followed a path through the surrounding jungle.

"The Sliani split off from contemporary society more than 200 years ago, when a prophet named Dralis had a visitation from their god," Petrallin told them. "Some Nvarati consider them an embarrassment. A throwback to an uncivilized age."

"But you don't?" Troi asked.

"They've always seemed harmless enough, if a little strange. We haven't had much contact with them for decades."

They passed a stretch of cleared farmland, lined with rows of crops. Soon they reached the outskirts of a village. There were no vehicles or other technology visible. The buildings here were simple wooden structures with little decoration. The streets were very narrow, and soon the hovercraft was forced to stop. "We'll walk from here," said Petralllin.

They continued on foot through the town, passing a few Sliani who regarded them with suspicion. They wore tunics of rough fabric, like Masang, but these Nvarati had dyed sections of their white fur in bright colors and shaven off patches of it in no discernable pattern. Some were holding large platters of fruits and vegetables. Others held leafy branches. All were hopping on one foot.

"I know it seems strange," said Petrallin. "But it's a religious sacrament to hop on one foot on the third and fourth day of the lunar cycle."

Worf glowered at him. "Are we expected to hop as well?"

"I don't think that will be necessary," the Second Minister told him.

They followed a group of Sliani, who led them to an open square. It was dominated by a large temple, the only stone building they had seen in the village. Sliani residents were hopping in from all around, approaching the temple and leaving platters of food by the door.

"Ah, yes. Today is the Feast Day of the All Powerful," said Petrallin.

Facing the temple was a statue,

at least eight feet tall, of a Nvarati figure. Picard stared, astonished to realize that he recognized its face.

"Q."

There was a horrified gasp from the Sliani around him. Several of them hissed at him. Petrallin quickly stepped forward. "It's considered blasphemy to say the name of the All Powerful." Then it occurred to him, "How do you even know what his name is?"

"We've encountered this being on several occasions," said Picard. "He appears to us in human form."

Troi asked, "This is the being who visited the Sliani prophet 200 years ago?"

Petrallin nodded. "As I understand it, he's appeared to his people two or three times since then as well. To issue proclamations about how to behave, how to worship him."

Picard looked around at the Sliani, their hair dyed and shaved, hopping to the temple to leave bountiful offerings. "Yes, I'm sure it amuses him greatly."

"Captain, we cannot allow him to continue toying with these people," said Worf.

"What would you have me do?" asked Picard. "Declare their god to be false?"

"But he *is* false."

"They wouldn't believe me even if I tried."

Troi said, "Is it really up to us to tell them who they should or shouldn't worship? The Rigellians regard a particular mountain as the embodiment of their god." She lowered her voice. "And Q is, in fact, an omnipotent being."

Picard considered this. "We can't interfere with the natural development of their society. It would be a gross violation of the Prime Directive."

"Even if he…" Worf jerked his head toward the statue. "…is already interfering with it? Telling them to sacrifice people?"

The door to the temple opened and a Nvarati woman came out. Her tunic was dyed sky blue and her fur was elaborately braided. All of the Sliani immediately touched their foreheads respectfully. "Must be the Grand Talik," said Petrallin.

Picard approached her. "I'm Captain Jean-Luc Picard," he said. "This is Lieutenant Worf and Counselor Deanna Troi."

The woman peered at them closely. "What manner of creatures are you?"

"I'm human. My companions are Klingon and Betazed. We represent an organization called the Federation of Planets."

She sniffed Picard, wrinkling her nose. "You may call me Tsulata. I'm the Grand Talik of my people."

"I'm very pleased to meet you," he said.

Tsulata glared at Petrallin. "Why have you come here? You're no believer."

He didn't mince words. "Is it true that you're sacrificing people to this god of yours?"

"Where did you hear that?"

"From one of your would-be victims."

She ruffled her fur in anger. "You must return her at once."

Picard faced the Grand Talik. "We understand that this is a new

SUDDENLY, THERE WAS A BRIGHT FLASH OF LIGHT AND EVERYONE FROZE IN PLACE. PICARD HEARD AN ALL-TOO-FAMILIAR VOICE.

practice of yours. When did the All Powerful command you to sacrifice your own citizens?"

"Do you question my interpretation of His teachings?" she demanded.

"We only seek to understand," said Troi.

Tstulata turned away from them and called, "Bring the offering."

Two Sliani emerged from the crowd, escorting a third man. He didn't struggle or object as they led him in front of the statue of Q. Tsulata reached into her tunic and pulled out a large knife.

Petrallin started forward. "This is absurd."

Tsulata gestured to another Sliani, who used a large branch to hit Petrallin on the back of the head,

knocking him out.

Worf stepped in to intervene, but Picard held him back. He tried addressing the Grand Talik again. "Please wait a moment. We can discuss…"

"No more delays!" she shouted. She approached the sacrificial victim, knife in hand. The Sliani stood quietly, awaiting his fate.

"Captain…" growled Worf.

Picard wrestled with his own conscience. But the Prime Directive was clear. "We can't interfere."

Tsulata raised the knife to strike. Suddenly, there was a bright flash of light and everyone froze in place. Everyone but Picard. He heard an all-too-familiar voice in his ear. "You were really going to stand by and watch her kill him, weren't you?"

Picard turned to find Q standing right beside him. "Stop this, Q."

"What if I told you there was another way to save that man's life, by offering yourself in his place? Or does your precious Prime Directive forbid that, too?"

"No one needs to die here. Tell them not to sacrifice people in your name."

"I don't remember asking them to do that," said Q. "What would I need with blood sacrifice?"

"Then stop it."

Q peered at him. "You still haven't answered my question. Would you take his place?"

Picard held his gaze. "No."

"How interesting! Not very noble, though, is it?" crowed Q. "What if it were five men? Ten? A hundred? What's your limit on self-sacrifice?"

He considered this. "I don't know," he said finally. "Is that what you want to hear?"

"You are continually fascinating, Mon Capitan. Wanting so badly to be better than you are."

"This is irrelevant. Tell them to stop the sacrifice."

"I'll consider it. But it is my Feast Day, after all. I do expect some gifts."

Picard took a deep breath. "What do you want?"

"Just a little worship. From the three of you." He nodded at Troi and Worf. "Kneel before me and swear your eternal loyalty to the All Powerful."

"Then you'll forbid blood sacrifice?"

Q smiled. "If I'm satisfied with your devotion."

He snapped his fingers and everyone who had been frozen came back to life. "Behold the All Powerful!" he declared. The Sliani immediately began making a loud whooping noise of praise. Tsulata did the same, momentarily backing away from her sacrificial victim.

"Q," growled Worf, and started toward him. Picard held him back.

"He's agreed to end the sacrifices," said the Captain. "If we kneel before him and swear loyalty."

Worf glared at Q. "I would rather die."

"We'll do it to save lives," Picard told him.

"That will only reinforce the idea that Q is a god," said Troi.

"I'm aware of that. But I don't see an alternative."

"Excellent." Q beamed at them.

Picard hesitated. Then he went on one knee. Troi followed suit. Worf remained standing. "Captain…"

"That's an order, Mr. Worf."

Q smiled and gestured toward the ground at his feet. The Klingon snarled, but finally obeyed his Captain and knelt.

"And?" Q prompted.

Picard glared at him. "I swear loyalty to the All Powerful."

Q gestured to the gathered Sliani. "All together now."

"What will you tell the First Minister about our application to the Federation?"

The Captain considered. "The Nvarati could strengthen their case if they were to reach out to their neighbors for an exchange of ideas."

Troi smiled. "Which might make the new generation of Sliani start to question their devotion to the All Powerful."

"Far be it from me to influence the cultural evolution of this world," Picard replied.

The group returned to the hovercraft, leaving the Sliani to celebrate the Feast Day of the All Powerful. Q watched them go.

"Until next time, Mon Capitan…"

Lisa Klink is a writer who has written episodes for *Star Trek: Voyager* and *Star Trek: Deep Space Nine*. She was also credited as writer for *Star Trek: The Experience – Borg Invasion 4D* and was credited as an executive story editor for season four of *Star Trek: Voyager*. Lisa has also written episodes for Gene Roddenberry's *Earth: Final Conflict, Martial Law, Buzz Lightyear of Star Command, Roswell, Painkiller Jane,* and *Hercules: The Legendary Journeys*. Lisa has written several novels, including *All In, All Gone* and *Evil to Burn*.

Artist Christian Rosado lives in Peru and has drawn for several Peruvian projects, plus *Taarna* for *Heavy Metal* and *The Saints* and *The Futurists* for *Allegiance Arts*.

> Q GESTURED TOWARD THE GROUND AT HIS FEET. THE KLINGON SNARLED, BUT FINALLY OBEYED HIS CAPTAIN AND KNELT.

The Captain, Worf, and Troi repeated the oath, along with Tsulata and everyone in the square. Q grinned, delighted. "Wonderful."

"Your turn," said Picard.

"Ah, yes." Q raised his arms and said grandly, "I hereby decree that no one shall be sacrificed in the name of the All Powerful."

Tsulata spoke up. "What about our livestock?"

"What about them?" asked Q.

"They're dying."

"Oh, is that all?" He snapped his fingers again. "Problem solved. Courtesy of your beloved All Powerful. Now bring me more of that candied fruit."

Picard, Worf, and Troi stood as the Sliani rushed forward with their offerings. Tsulata tucked the knife back into her waistband. The would-be sacrificial victim looked both stunned and relieved at the abrupt turn of events.

Troi went to Petrallin, who was groggily starting to sit up. "Are you all right?"

"I think so…"

"Let's get you back to the city," said Picard, and helped the man stand.

A *STAR TREK: DEEP SPACE NINE* STORY

A Night In

STORY: UNA MCCORMACK
ILLUSTRATION: LOUIE DE MARTINIS

Elim Garak – spy, exile, saboteur, tailor-on-hiatus and present jailbird – never slept particularly deeply, and so was easily woken in the early hours of the morning (station time) by what was best described as an "altercation." Rolling over to sit on the side of his bed, he peered out through the force barrier and watched with interest and some amusement as Odo and one of his security team attempted to wrestle a single, resisting prisoner across the room toward the cells. There was a slight cut on Odo's left cheek, below the eye... And what, Garak wondered, would the constable make of that? Injury; frailty; the hard, material consequences of a hostile universe. None of these had troubled Odo in the past. Now he was as fragile as the rest of them.

The prisoner, realizing his destination, struggled harder, and yelled, "You'll never take me alive!" This battle cry turned to be his last slurred hurrah; the effort took his remaining strength. His legs gave way beneath him, and, slumping into the arms of the security guard, he began to snore, loudly.

Odo, gently rubbing the graze on his cheek, looked past Garak at the other two cells. They were full. Two Ferengi, caught trying to cheat on the *dabo* wheel in one; a Nausicaan who had attempted to smuggle a deciliter of biomimetic gel onto the station in the other; and, with him, Chayo Trusi, the station's resident drunk and other most regular occupant of the holding cells – if one did not count Garak himself, in the third cell, currently enjoying his fourth month detained at Sisko's pleasure for the minor misdemeanors of sabotage and assault... Quite how he'd avoided the charge of attempted genocide Garak was not entirely sure, but everyone seemed ready to let that one pass, even Odo. For this reason alone (there were many others), Garak could hardly refuse the constable's next request.

"Garak," said Odo. "I'll have to put him in with you."

With a sigh, Garak stood up, crossed to the other bed, and began to gather his possessions. Astonishing how quickly clutter accumulated, but then there were many hours in the day, and visits from Ziyal, Bashir, and Rom only filled a few. Garak piled up his clothes and padds and sewing and *kotra* set and data rods and various other miscellanea, took them over to his side of the cell, and shoved the lot unceremoniously under his bed. He could kill a few minutes tomorrow sorting them out again, he supposed.

"I'm sorry about this," said Odo.

"I was at no point under the impression that this was a hotel, constable."

"He'll only be here till the morning, I assure you."

Garak shrugged. At least it was a change. He watched Odo switch off the force barrier, and then the constable and the security officer started to haul their prisoner into the cell. Garak helped them get him onto the bed, where the cell's new

inhabitant rolled over to face the wall, gave a penetratingly loud snort, and went back to sleep. As Odo and the guard went back out of the cell, Garak tapped his cheek with his fingertip. "Do get that cut checked, constable."

Odo, with a grunt, raised the force barrier again, and glared round at the other cells. Chayo had slept through the whole interruption, Garak noted, although the Ferengi were chittering away, and the Nausicaan was loudly cursing his captors.

"Be quiet!" Odo growled, a man whose day had by now gone on far too long. There was a general reduction in noise, and the constable turned back to Garak. "I'll see you at breakfast."

"I shall look forward to it."

Odo gave the new arrival one, last withering look. "I hope you sleep well."

"Oh, I always sleep well," lied Garak.

* * *

Famous last words. After Odo left, killing the lights as he went, the Ferengi resumed their chatter until the Nausicaan threatened, loudly, that he would rip off their ears. The Nausicaan continued shouting until

Not a chance. Garak's only regret was his lack of success; that his attempt to deal with the Founders once and for all had ended in a rather unceremonious beating from Commander Worf. At least Garak had landed a punch or two of his own. Not bad after five years' exile. But the Founders remained, and their threat to Cardassia had been issued, and only Garak knew the extent of their antipathy, the sheer *viciousness* with which the Female Changeling had issued her threat… Sometimes, particularly when he was on the edge of sleep, he would relive the moment, and his blood would run cold… *"They're dead. You're dead, Cardassia is dead. Your people were doomed the moment they attacked us…"*

Garak woke, suddenly, and piercingly conscious of being watched. He took a deep and calming breath, reminded himself that he could not be reached, not in here, and turned his head – to see his cellmate staring at him. Slowly, he inched his hand round to retrieve the fabric cutter concealed beneath the pillow. Odo didn't know about this. An uncharacteristic lapse on the constable's part, but solidity had made him markedly less capable and

GARAK'S ONLY REGRET WAS HIS LACK OF SUCCESS; THAT HIS ATTEMPT TO DEAL WITH THE FOUNDERS HAD ENDED IN A BEATING FROM WORF.

Garak insinuated, quietly, that he would rip off his arms. After that, the room began to settle. Garak lay back in the darkness, completely awake, and listened to the snores of his cellmate.

Boredom had always been one of Garak's sorest trials living on this cursed station, and a period of confinement only exacerbated the problem. Nothing to do other than contemplate the decisions that had brought him here… He suspected that this was part of the point; a typically sanctimonious attempt by the Federation to make him repent his crimes and sorrowfully conclude that their way was best.

Garak was certainly not above taking advantage of this new state of affairs.

"That won't do you any good," said his cellmate.

"Excuse me?"

"The cutter under your pillow. It won't do you any good."

"No?"

"No," said his cellmate. "You can't kill me."

Garak pulled back his hand and sat up on the bed. Curiosity was getting the better of him. Always one of his flaws. He eyed the other man. Who *was* this, exactly? Was it someone sent to deal with him? Had the Founders discovered his part in Tain's assault on their home

endless wars. I have troubles of my own, you know—"

It was best, Garak thought, to humor him in these delusions. "You're not, presumably, bound to stay," said Garak. "If you're omnipotent. Why don't you leave?"

"Leave?"

"You could… release the force barrier? "

"Too trivial."

"Transport yourself elsewhere?"

"Too bothersome."

"Remake the timeline?"

That caught his attention. "You know," he said, "I might just do that…"

"If you could hurry up," said Garak, "then I might just still get some sleep."

"Huh. I wonder how you'd like it."

"Like what?" said Garak.

"Omniscience. Invincibility. Complete control."

He spoke as if they were curses. There was, in fact, nothing in the entire universe that Garak would like more. "Are you making me an offer?"

There was a moment's pause. The man smiled – rather cruelly, Garak thought, and he would know. "You'd like that, wouldn't you?" said the man. "They've got other plans for you."

"Who?" said Garak.

"The Founders. They want you to live. They want you to see how it ends." The man eyed Garak. "It's not pretty."

Garak suddenly felt rather cold; colder than usual.

"You don't know who I am, do you?" said the man. "What I am? Why I'm here?"

"Who are you?" breathed Garak. "*What* are you?"

The man gave another crooked smile.

"All right then," said Garak, "why *are* you here?"

"The same as you," he said. "There's a war, and my enemies are in power." The man stopped himself. "No, you've

not quite got to that part yet, have you? Well, it's not as if you haven't worked out what's coming. All those hours alone, pondering your choices, working through the logical outcomes, as if you're playing a giant *kotra* board…"

I would like to kill you, thought Garak.

"You can't," said the man. "I'm immortal."

He clicked his fingers—

* * *

—And they were there, like that, on Cardassia Prime, and the sun was setting. And if it was possible to feel the absence of something when so certainly, so viscerally, and so immediately in its presence – then Garak lost Cardassia all over again. The air thick with the heavy perfume of *ithian* blossom and the acrid tang of skimmer fuel; closer to hand the bitter scent of *gelat* wafting from an open window… He knew immediately where he was; on a walkway in East Torr, the trams rattling by underneath; the commuter crowd flowing past, people – many, many people – exactly like him and were not in any way alien…

A click of the fingers…

—And he saw everything again, burned black and ruined; heard the awful silence of the millions of dead, and he knew – immediately, and terribly – how close this end was, how little chance there was that this fate could be escaped… He turned on the other man, angry, and desperate.

"You could stop this, couldn't you?" whispered Garak. "If you wanted."

"Perhaps," said his cellmate. "Yes. Of course. If I wanted."

"But you won't."

"No."

"I'm not going to beg," said Garak. "If that's what you want—"

"Beg? I should think not."

world all those years ago? Had they marked him for special attention? "And is there any particular reason," asked Garak, "*why* I can't kill you?"

"Because I'm immortal."

Garak slumped back against the wall. Not an assassin, then. Just a drunk.

"You don't believe me," said the other man.

"Well, no."

"Immortal, omnipotent, and omniscient. And no – I've not been sent to kill you, by the Founders, the Romulans, the Central Command, or anyone else."

Garak blinked.

"I told you I was omniscient," said the other man, listlessly. He didn't seem particularly enchanted by this ability.

"Or else you've read my file," said Garak.

"I did that too. It was considerably less interesting than you'd like it to be."

"Now that," said Garak, tartly, "is certainly not true."

"It filled a couple of nano-seconds, I'll grant you that." The man stretched out on the bed. "How wearying you people are! Your tiresome politics, your

SLOWLY, GARAK INCHED HIS HAND ROUND TO RETRIEVE THE FABRIC CUTTER CONCEALED BENEATH HIS PILLOW. ODO DIDN'T KNOW ABOUT THIS.

"Then help. Help me!" Garak held out his hands to encompass everything he loved. "Help *Cardassia*…"

"Humanity is more my interest," said the man, coolly. "On balance, I think I'd rather see *them* win." He clicked his fingers once more, and they were back in the cell, each on their own side of the little room. Garak sat, head in hands, still exiled and lost.

"Why don't you leave?" asked his cellmate.

"What?" said Garak, looking up.

"That force field – it's hardly a barrier to you, is it?"

Garak tilted his head; part-admission, part-denial.

"You could walk out of here, whenever you chose," said the man. "More than that. A man like you – resourceful, clever. A new face, a new identity – you could start again, wherever and however you chose. But you don't. So… why not?"

"It's not as simple as that," said Garak.

The man did not reply at once.

The memory of Cardassia Prime – its sounds and scents and colors, its warm and all-encompassing embrace – lay between them. "No," said the man, after a while. "I see that now."

He clicked his fingers once more. Everything went dark.

* * *

Garak woke, suddenly, to bright lights and an empty cell. Odo was lurking beyond the force barrier, arms folded, rocking back and forward on the soles of his feet.

"You slept well," said the constable.

"For once," said Garak, wondering if he had their guest to thank for that. At least it was something. He nodded toward the other bed. "Where's our friend?"

"He had a berth on a Bajoran freighter this morning. I sent him on his way."

"And the others?"

"Fined the Ferengi. Handed the Nausicaan over to Starfleet said Odo.

Garak, startled, put down his coffee mug. "I beg your pardon?"

"You're not fooling me. I know you could walk out of your cell at any time."

Garak looked round the little space. "It's… restful?" he offered.

Odo snorted. "Hardly. So why do you stay?"

"You know why," said Garak, softly. "I stay for the same reason as you." And he watched, with keen interest, as the goosebumps prickled along Odo's arm and the small hairs stood to attention.

Quickly, Odo collected himself. "And what do you think that might be?" he growled.

Garak saw, in his mind's eye, the vision of the previous night, of Cardassia – dead and burned – and felt again how little time there was left; how little room there was left for maneuver. If there was anything he could do, it would be done, and there was no escaping that. No click of the fingers; no benign godchild to dispense favors and fortune – only himself, and whatever could be done with whatever was to hand.

"Oh Odo," said Garak, wearily, "where else exactly would we go?" ⚓

"WHO ARE YOU?" BREATHED GARAK. "WHAT ARE YOU?" THE MAN GAVE ANOTHER CROOKED SMILE.

Intelligence."

"A busy morning," said Garak.

"And I've still not had breakfast," replied Odo, pointedly.

"My apologies for oversleeping," Garak said.

Odo, placated, went through the usual morning routine: replicating breakfast; setting the trays down on a small table; releasing Garak to join him. Odo liked his rituals. He sat and watched as Odo put too much sugar into his *raktajino*. Someone should tell him about the consequences of that. The cut on his cheek was gone, at least; only the faint pale patch left by the dermal regeneration process that would soon fade. Odo took his first sip of coffee, then turned his attention to his toast, buttering it precisely, cutting it into perfect quarters. The same every morning. There was comfort in certainties.

"Why don't you leave, Garak?"

■ **Dr Una McCormack is a *New York Times* bestselling science fiction author, based in Cambridge, UK. She has written more than a dozen novels set in franchises such as *Doctor Who*, *Star Trek: Deep Space Nine*, and *Star Trek: Discovery*. Her audio work with Big Finish has been set in licensed properties such as *Doctor Who* and *Blake's 7*. Her 2020 release, *Star Trek: Picard* novel "The Last Best Hope," became a *USA Today* bestseller, and her most recent book, *The Autobiography of Mr Spock*, was published by Titan in September 2021.**

■ **Louie De Martinis is an illustrator and comic book artist, living in Montreal, Canada. He has also worked in the animation industry on background design, storyboards and development art. He has drawn for *Penny Dreadful* by Titan Books and *Star Wars Insider* magazine.**

The Offer

STORY: JAMES SWALLOW

*(Author's note: this story takes place in 2150, months before the events of the **Star Trek: Enterprise** episode "Broken Bow")*

lthough it was behavior that wasn't becoming of a Starfleet officer, Jonathan Archer vented his annoyance by slamming the shuttlepod's hatch closed behind him as he climbed aboard it.

He dropped heavily into the passenger seat behind the pilot and released a long, slow sigh, trying to get his bad mood under rein.

"Are you all right, Commander?" The pilot didn't turn around to ask the question, his hands moving over the controls. "Tough day?"

"You don't know the half of it, Lieutenant," Archer replied, more tersely than he intended. "Let's go."

"On the way."

Archer felt the shift in gravity as the craft rotated into launch position, then the rocking motion as it fell from the orbital platform and into open space. He looked up, out of the small portal in the hatch, watching the platform recede.

The floating complex they had departed was a series of small cylinders attached to a central spindle, the control center for a nearby cluster of skeletal dry docks. Beneath Archer's viewpoint, Earth cast a blue-white glow across the scene, illuminating the craft in the docks, in their different stages of construction.

His eyes were drawn to one particular vessel, the steel-colored saucer of its primary hull already finished, its twin pylons and engine nacelles yet to be fitted into place.

Enterprise. The ship's name was almost on his lips, but Archer couldn't bring himself to say it aloud. He had the horrible sense that if he did, he would forever be denied it.

The view was magnificent, but it did nothing to cool Archer's temper. It was as if the universe was mocking him.

A warning tone sounded and the shuttlepod rocked. Archer almost bumped his head on the panel and his attention snapped back to the pilot. "Easy on the stick, mister!"

"My apologies." The dark-haired pilot nodded toward something out past the cockpit canopy. "I had to course correct, because of *them*. They don't like human ships coming too close."

Archer looked up and saw the alien vessel looming large as they passed underneath it. Built of a shimmering, coppery metal, the sleek starship had the blade-like hull and circular ring array that was common to all Vulcan interstellar craft. "It's a *Suurok*-class. One of the High Command's top-line ships."

"I hear rumors they can make Warp 7."

"It's not a rumor," said Archer, failing to keep the bitterness out of his tone.

"And here's humanity, struggling to break Warp 5!" The pilot gave a derisive snort. "Hardly seems fair. Earth and Vulcan are supposed to be allies, but they hoard all their technology."

"I don't disagree." Archer frowned. For years, up through the trials of the NX test program and into the development of Starfleet's newest class of starships, he had carried the torch lit by his father Henry and Zefram Cochrane, the inventor of warp drive. The goal was to take humanity to the stars, but since First Contact, at every step the Vulcans had been there to pour cold water on Starfleet's ambitions. Their idea of collaboration was to enforce a list of everything humans could *not* do, rather than offer anything in the way of material help.

To say Archer resented the patronizing, judgmental attitude of the aliens was putting it mildly. He'd grown up watching his father labor to make the Warp 5 engine a reality, and he would always carry the sorrow of knowing Henry Archer did not live long enough to see it become reality. Had the Vulcans been true partners in their alliance with Earth, things might have gone differently.

And now all that long-simmering antipathy boiled back to the surface. Archer's foul mood was a result of the meeting he had just left; it had been framed as a discussion with Admiral Forrest, but when he arrived and saw the acerbic Vulcan ambassador Soval was present, Archer knew it was something much worse.

"What did Soval say this time?" asked the pilot. "Let me guess. He

THE GOAL WAS TO TO TAKE HUMANITY TO THE STARS, BUT SINCE FIRST CONTACT, AT EVERY STEP THE VULCANS HAD BEEN THERE TO POUR COLD WATER ON STARFLEET'S AMBITIONS.

told you humans aren't ready for deep space."

Archer hadn't said anything aloud, and yet the lieutenant seemed to pluck his thoughts from out of the air. "Something like that."

"What does he know? Vulcans! All that logic and raised eyebrows. They act like they possess the secrets of the universe, but they're just as limited and clueless as every other lifeform!" The pilot snorted again.

That wasn't all that Soval had said, of course. Archer had heard Vulcans insist that humanity *wasn't ready* his entire life, so much so that he hardly registered it anymore. But he hadn't been prepared for the demand the ambassador laid on the table.

Vulcan considers that Commander Archer is not a fitting choice for promotion to captaincy of the NX-01 Enterprise *at this time.* Soval hadn't even looked him the eye when he said it. *An older, more experienced officer… One with less adventurous proclivities… Would be preferable.*

It was damned presumptuous of Soval to try to influence Forrest's upcoming decision so openly, and while the final choice would be the admiral's to make, it didn't help Archer's case to have the Vulcans show zero confidence in him. Soval had dismissively suggested that Archer might possibly take a first officer's post on *Enterprise*, but he had been waiting too long and worked too hard to let his career take a retrograde step.

Of course, there were other good starships out there that needed a captain – Archer knew he could get command of an older *Freedom*-class boat if he asked for it – but none of them were *Enterprise*. The newest ship, with the newest engine, *his father's engine*. For the NX-01 to launch without him in the center seat… It felt like a failure of everything he had been working toward.

"Ever wondered what you might do if you could get a look inside that ship's engineering core?" The pilot nodded in the direction of Soval's vessel.

Something about the question rang an odd note with Archer.

"What's your name, Lieutenant?"

"Quebec, sir. With a *Q*."

Archer glanced up at the elegant Vulcan ship. "Well, Mister Quebec, you want my honest answer?"

"Oh, indeed."

Archer gave a rueful chuckle, amused at the idea. "I would grab everything that's not nailed down!"

"Really?" The lieutenant took his hands off the controls and pivoted in his chair, turning to face Archer for the first time. The man had a sly smile and the kind of glint in his eye that Archer associated with card sharps and con-men. He raised a hand. "And why not?"

The hairs on the back of Archer's neck stood up as the pilot snapped his fingers-

-a white flash engulfed everything, and then-

-They were somewhere else.

Another starship. Archer was a veteran spacer and by experience he knew the feel of artificial gravity and recycled atmosphere common to any space vessel, no matter its origins. But there was more he recognized –higher gravity, an arid taste of blood-warm air. He stood in the middle of a curving corridor lit in red-orange shades. *On a Vulcan ship.*

Years before, Archer had been a guest aboard a *Maymora*-class cruiser at the behest of the Vulcan High Command, largely a tourist for the duration. But he had never forgotten the alien environment on the vessel, and his skin prickled with the recollection.

"How…?" He found the pilot lounging against a bulkhead, arms folded across his chest. "Was that

…THERE WERE OTHER GOOD STARSHIPS OUT THERE THAT NEEDED A CAPTAIN — BUT NONE OF THEM WERE THE *ENTERPRISE*.

"I DON'T UNDERSTAND..." ARCHER'S QUESTION DIED IN HIS THROAT AS HE CAUGHT SIGHT OF HIS REFLECTION IN THE PORTAL.

some sort of matter transporter?"

"Some sort," sniffed the other man, as if he was talking to a dim child.

Suddenly, Archer sensed movement behind. To his shock, a pair of Vulcans in form-fitting jumpsuits walked past, intent on some errand. He tensed, expecting them to demand he account for his presence, but one of them gave a nod of greeting and both carried on as if nothing was amiss.

Archer went to a large transparent portal in the wall of the corridor and looked out into space. Beyond, he saw the curve of the Earth, the office complex and dry-docks, and then with a start, he found the silver dart of the shuttlepod he had been aboard only moments ago.

The smaller craft drifted alongside, keeping station with the alien ship.

"Don't worry about them," said the pilot. "They're not going to set off any red alerts, as long as you don't do anything foolish."

"I don't understand…" Archer's question died in his throat as he caught sight of his reflection – and that of the pilot's – in the portal. While to his eyes, both of them remained in Starfleet-standard uniforms, in the reflection each man was an alien iteration of himself, complete with upswept eyebrows and elfin, pointed ears. "Oh…boy."

"Amusing, isn't it?" The other man chuckled. "You and I see one another as we are, but these Vulcans see us as their fellows. And I've taken the liberty of tweaking their

perceptions so that the moment they're out of sight, they'll forget they ever laid eyes on us."

Archer rounded on him, struggling to regain some control of the situation. "You did this? What the hell *are* you, Quebec?"

"Well, I'm not from Canada, that's a fact." He smirked. "Call me Q. It's far less formal." He walked past Archer, beckoning him to follow. "Come, come, Jonathan. Things to see, things to do…"

"I'm not going anywhere," Archer insisted, "not without some explanation!"

Q gave a theatrical sigh. "Can't you just take something on faith, for once in your life?"

"That's not how I work."

Q saw the hard look in Archer's eyes. "Oh, very well, you'll continue be testy otherwise…" He scowled. "Whenever I deal with a lesser being, I have to do this…" Q took a deep breath and went into a speech that he had clearly given many times over. "I am a member of a race of non-corporeal life from beyond what your limited mind conceives of as space-time. We possess infinite, omnipotent powers, to the extent that matter, reality and time are fully malleable in our hands." He gave a small bow. "I am, and we are, *the Q*."

"Right." Archer's tone was flat. "Infinitely powerful, but not every inventive with names." He looked the other man up and down. "I guess I can't argue with that, based on what I've seen so far. So tell me, what do you do with that power?"

Q's smile widened into a grin. "Oh, Jonny. I *enjoy* it." He started walking, and reluctantly, Archer fell in step with him.

"Know this right now, if you're here to stir up trouble between Earth and Vulcan, I won't allow it."

Q gave him a sideways glance. "But you hate them!"

"I don't *like* them," Archer corrected. "But I won't judge an entire species just because the ones I've met so far are, well, jackasses." He focused on Q. "So why are you doing this? You like screwing around with lesser beings for fun?"

"You're quick, I like that," said Q. "I'd be lying if I said humans aren't interesting… But the reason I'm giving you this opportunity is because we want to see how your kind might succeed if given… A *boost*."

"What opportunity?" said Archer, as they reached a heavy door at the end of the corridor. "Is this some kind of test?"

"All things are," said Q. He waved at the air, and the door opened to reveal the most incredible machine Archer had ever seen.

The warp core of the Vulcan starship was elegant and perfect in its mechanical execution, a streamlined construct of glowing cylinders, shimmering rods and rotating hoops. Just seeing it for the first time, Archer had flashes of insight into how the aliens had refined the technology of warp theory and matter-antimatter systems. It was an amazing piece of work, as much art as craft, and he wanted to know everything about it.

"Close your mouth," Q said quietly. "You'll attract attention."

"No human has ever been allowed to see a Vulcan warp core," he whispered, moving carefully along one of the maintenance catwalks suspended above the pulsing intermix chamber. "They didn't want us learning their tricks." Archer traced the components of the system, picking out what had to be phase inducers, plasma conduits and the central dilithium crystal module.

For a moment, he forgot the circumstances that had brought him here, his mind fizzing with possibilities. Even from this cursory examination, he gathered insights that could translate into improvements for existing Warp 5 technology.

"What do we have here?" Q plucked something from the top of a nearby control console and tossed it to Archer.

Archer caught the device and turned it over in his hand. The Vulcan version of a digital padd, as he paged through it he realized he was looking at the full technical manual for *Suurok*-class starship's propulsion system. The warp field equations contained in it alone could revolutionize the design of the NX-01 and advance Starfleet's warp drive program by a decade, at a single stroke.

"Tempted?" said Q. "Take it. And don't fret, I'll make sure no-one knows it went missing."

Archer gripped the pad. Suddenly, it felt impossibly heavy, as if made of neutronium. "Suppose I do. What then?"

"Every choice is a test, Jonathan," said Q. "This is yours."

For a long moment, Archer hung on the possibilities before him. "I want this," he admitted. "I really do. We deserve this. My father deserved it."

"Then take it," repeated Q, "and change the future."

"No." At length, Archer placed the pad back where it belonged. "I appreciate the offer, but we've come this far alone. Humanity needs to do this ourselves."

"Are you absolutely certain? This is a one-time deal."

Archer smiled. "I never cheated on a test in my life. I'm not going to start now. I'd rather see humanity on a long road to get where we're going, than take a short-cut." He shook his head. "No offence, but I don't want to put myself in debt to a god-like being. I've read the classics, I know how those bargains turn out."

"Disappointing," said Q, more to himself than in reply. "I thought if I wound back the clock a few centuries before Jean-Luc, I'd find someone more free-spirited, but you're not that different, are you? Starfleet officers are all the same, under the skin. So very principled."

"Who's *Jean-Luc*?"

Q laughed. "I'll tell him you said that, he'll be terribly put out." He raised his hand. "I think it's best for all of us that I edit this little encounter out of the timeline. Just in case you remember something you're not supposed to."

"You'll wipe my memory?"

"More like re-set causality at a quantum level, but yes."

"One question before you do," Archer insisted.

"You'll get your bold little *Enterprise*," said Q, anticipating the human's query. "And that name will know more adventures than you can imagine." Then the trickster smiled again. "But remember what they say, Jonathan. *Be careful what you wish for*."

Q snapped his fingers-
-*and a white flash engulfed everything-*

■ **James Swallow is a *New York Times*, *Sunday Times* and *Amazon* #1 bestselling author of over fifty novels, and a BAFTA-nominated scriptwriter with over a million books in print worldwide. He is the creator of the Marc Dane action thriller series, and has written for franchises such as *Star Trek*, *24*, *Marvel* and several high-profile videogames. He lives and works in London.**

A STAR TREK VOYAGER STORY

Seven > Seven

STORY: GREG COX
ILLUSTRATION: CHRISTIAN ROSADO

esistance is futile."

"That remains to be seen."

Seven of Nine, of late a crew member aboard the U.S.S. *Voyager,* faced her none-too distant past amidst a rugged alien landscape. Seven of Nine, Tertiary Adjunct of Unimatrix Zero One, a fully-assimilated Borg drone, coolly regarded her from several meters away. Mottled gray flesh, darkly veined, attested to the drone's membership in the Collective, as did her matte-black body armor, protruding optical implant, loops of exterior tubing, and harsh contemptuous tone.

"No uncertainty exists. You have become small, weak, diminished. A mere individual."

Perhaps, Seven conceded. Staring at the drone was like looking backwards in time at a distorted reflection of herself – or was she the distortion? She was torn between admiration and, curiously, revulsion. "And you are?" she asked, already knowing the answer, but stalling for time.

"We are Borg."

It advanced toward Seven at a steady, implacable pace. By design, the rocky terrain, situated upon a wide granite ledge partway up a nameless mountain, beneath a clear vermillion sky, was neutral ground, offering no advantage to either combatant, resembling neither the sleek corridors of *Voyager* nor the austere interior of a Borg cube. They had the desolate battleground to themselves, with no allies or reinforcements to call upon. The temperature and humidity were an equitable mean between human and Borg preferences. Not unlike Seven herself, now that she thought of it.

This was no time for irrelevant musings, however. Seven warily clocked the drone's advance, overcoming any instinctive urge to retreat. Although her own strength and endurance exceeded those of purely organic humans, the drone's full complement of synthetic implants rendered it stronger still. Speed, agility, and surprise were Seven's only possible advantages against the drone. She needed to strike first – and swiftly.

Her Starfleet-issue phaser set at maximum, she fired at the drone, hoping to kill or at least incapacitate it before it could adapt to this specific attack. The crimson beam scorched the air between them, only to be blocked by the shimmering green radiance of the drone's personal force field. To Seven's dismay, the beam failed to damage the drone at all. She suddenly regretted not presetting the phaser to automatically modulate its frequencies, but that had previously struck her as unfairly tipping the contest in her favor; it had felt like "cheating."

Not that the drone concerned itself with such caveats.

"We are Borg. We have adapted to all known Federation weapons and tactics. You cannot defeat us."

"I will require proof of that assertion." Seven backed away from the drone, attempting to recalibrate the phaser's settings as expeditiously as possible. Despite her brave front, however, she feared the drone was not inaccurate in its assessment. How could a mere individual prevail against the Collective, as embodied by her former self?

"Your thought processes are disorganized. You lack clarity."

"Possibly, but your conversation leaves much to be desired."

"Conversation is irrelevant."

The barren ledge offered little in the way of protection. With no crags, boulders, or ravine to hide behind, Seven could only scramble to keep out of reach of the oncoming drone. Intent on her adversary, she slipped on a patch of loose scree, twisting her ankle. She winced, but managed to avoid falling. The injury slowed her, allowing the drone to gain ground on her. Unlike many Borg, the drone had not had an arm replaced by a multi-purpose prosthetic limb; its specific tasks had required the dexterity of two humanoid hands. Seven found herself grateful that her earlier incarnation was not equipped with rotating saws and high-temperature plasma cutters. Small blessings, as her new Collective aboard *Voyager* might say.

She used her own hand, reinforced by its exo-scaffolding, to fire again at the drone. Her heart sank as the modulated beam only staggered the drone for a moment.

"We anticipated your tactic, based on past encounters with Starfleet. It is no longer effective against us."

I know, Seven thought, losing hope. The drone closed on her and, limping, Seven found herself backed up against a sheer cliff face. Gravity trapped her on the ledge. Injection tubules extended from the drone's wrist.

"Retreat is futile. You will reassimilated."

Seven conceded defeat. "Computer. End program."

The ledge vanished, taking the drone with it. An empty holodeck left her alone with the realization that her past had beaten her . . . again.

*   *   *

"And the purpose of this particular simulation would be?" the Emergency Medical Hologram asked.

Seven hesitated before answering. She had reported to Sickbay for one of her regular mandatory checkups, but the Doctor had noted her injured ankle, along with various minor bruises and abrasions stemming from her recent activities in the holodeck, so it appeared she had little choice

but to confide in him. She regretted that she'd not had time to regenerate in her alcove before this encounter.

"To demonstrate that my regained humanity – your handiwork, Doctor – had not significantly lessened me . . . or my ability to defend myself."

She declined to mention that such concerns had been heightened by her recent capture and abuse at the hands of the Hirogen while attempting to stabilize an interstellar relay station. To find herself helpless and at the mercy of her captors – members of Species 478, to be precise – had been disconcerting. Once Borg, she was unaccustomed to feeling so . . . vulnerable.

"I see." The EMH employed a subcutaneous tissue regenerator to repair her ankle. "And the results so far?"

"Unsatisfactory. The drone has vanquished me nineteen out of nineteen times."

Or would have had she'd allowed the simulations to reach their inevitable outcomes; Seven had seen no need to endure even a virtual reassimilation once it became obvious that, well, further resistance was futile.

"Perhaps you're looking at this the wrong way," the EMH suggested.

"Combat exercises aside, it may be that you've gained more than you lost by becoming an individual. Even if you're not the unstoppable assimilation machine you once were, is that such a bad thing?"

Seven appreciated the Doctor's generous sentiments, but the drone's blunt assessment echoed in her memory, as once the myriad voices of the Collective had:

You have become small, weak, diminished.

"I am . . . uncertain," she admitted.

"In that case, let me propose an alternative approach." The EMH completed his repairs to her damaged ligaments. "Why don't I monitor your next simulation? Maybe another pair of eyes can provide a different perspective and ascertain why that holographic drone keeps gaining the upper hand."

"Thank you, Doctor, but that is unnecessary. This is not your concern."

"I beg to differ. As you pointed out just a moment ago, I am indeed responsible for removing and/or replacing the majority of your Borg implants."

"Eighty-two percent," she noted.

"More or less," he said,

[SEVEN] COULD NOT HELP ENVYING THE DRONE'S RELENTLESS PURPOSE AND INVULNERABILITY.

grimacing. "The point being that I have a professional and personal interest in helping you cope with any consequences from those procedures, including your present crisis of confidence. I would be remiss as your physician if I did *not* attempt to remedy your concerns."

Seven considered his offer. Certainly, she had reached an impasse in her own efforts. Conducting the trial for a twentieth time without any significant variations was unlikely to yield a different result, let alone any pertinent new insights. She tested her ankle and found it sound.

"You make a persuasive case, Doctor, but I must insist that you refrain from coming to my aid against the drone. The exercise is pointless if I cannot defeat it without assistance."

"Not to worry," he assured her. "Far be it from me to come between you and you."

*   *   *

"Resistance is futile."

"So I have been informed."

Seven experienced a very human sense of déjà vu as the simulation recommenced, albeit with a revised setting. She had instructed the computer to randomize the environment, with a narrow range of parameters, so that she could not gain an advantage by growing more familiar with the terrain over the course of repeated trials. As a result, she now confronted the drone atop a bleak, moonlit mesa overlooking a vast desert of glittering crystal shards. Auroral lights, reminiscent of the sickly green glow of Borg technology, shimmered overhead.

Despite the imminent threat posed by the drone, Seven risked glancing at the EMH, who stood off to one side, serving as an audience of one.

"Don't mind me," he said. "Just pretend I'm not here."

Easier said than done. It occurred to her that the Doctor could prove an unwelcome distraction. The drone, on the other hand, was oblivious to his presence. As intended, it could not see or hear him, not even with its enhanced senses.

"We are Borg. You will rejoin the Collective."

As always, the drone marched toward Seven, who did not bother to fire her phaser at the drone this time around; a full range of settings, from stun to disintegrate, had been ineffective in previous trials, no matter how quickly or accurately she targeted her opponent. Instead she employed the phaser to carve a deep trench between her and the drone, while simultaneously scanning the environment for any possible strategic advantage. Patches of scrub dotted the mesa. Perhaps she could distract the drone by setting the sparse flora ablaze?

"You cannot impede me." A flickering green force field manifested beneath the drone's boots, allowing it to traverse the vacant space above the trench. "We are Borg. We are inevitable."

Seven found that difficult to dispute. She could not help envying the drone's relentless purpose and invulnerability. This version of herself would not have been so easily taken hostage by Species 478 . . . .

In desperation, she flung the phaser at the drone's skull, hoping that a physical projectile would fare better than an energy blast, but the drone effortlessly deflected the weapon with a perfectly-timed sweep of its arm, causing the phaser to go flying off the edge of the mesa. A glowing red sensor blinked upon the drone's protruding ocular implant, reminding Seven of its superior vision. Small wonder it had so easily calculated the missile's trajectory.

"Your primitive attacks are pointless. We surpass you in all respects."

"Don't listen to it!" the EMH called out. "It's another Borg. You're unique!"

Seven feared that was insufficient.

Then the impossible happened: the drone turned her head toward the EMH.

"You are human," the holographic drone said of the holographic Doctor. It veered away from Seven to advance on the newcomer. "We will add your distinctiveness to our own."

SEVEN DID NOT UNDERSTAND WHAT WAS HAPPENING. WAS THE HOLODECK MALFUNCTIONING?

Seven did not understand what was happening. Was the holodeck malfunctioning? The drone should be unable to perceive the Doctor in any way.

"Computer. End program."

"Negative," an artificial voice replied. "Authorization denied."

"Unacceptable," Seven declared to no avail. With no time to locate a manual access panel, she looked on with alarm as the drone closed on the EMH, who retreated fearfully. He held up his hands in a futile effort to deter his attacker.

"No! Stay back! My individuality is one of my most sterling qualities. I'm a doctor, not a drone!"

"Irrelevant." Her injection tubules extended.

"Borg!" Seven shouted to the drone from across the trench. "I'm your objective, not him. Assimilate me if you can."

"We are already you. Reassimilating you is mere redundancy. It will wait until after we have assimilated this other individual."

"Please, don't!" the EMH whimpered. "Keep your tubules away from me!"

Panic contorted his features, his obvious distress spurring Seven

to action. Was it possible the safety protocols were malfunctioning as well? She understood that such potentially dire emergencies had been known to occur on Starfleet vessels.

"Leave him!"

Backing up to get a running start, she bounded over the trench and tackled the drone, her momentum carrying them both off the mesa. Gravity seized them and they plunged toward the jagged wasteland below, grappling in midair as they fell. The drone's tubules stabbed Seven's throat, causing her to cry out in pain.

"Resistance is futile."

"Irrelevant."

Locked in the drone's grasp, and vice versa, Seven seized the Borg's projecting eyepiece and savagely yanked it out with her augmented right hand. Sparks flared from the gaping eye socket. The drone twitched and convulsed. Its organic eye rolled upward until only the whites were seen. An unintelligible rattle escaped its lips.

Seven smiled grimly as the desert floor seemed to rush up at her as though launched from a shuttle bay. Then, right before the moment of impact, the crystal expanse blinked out of existence and she landed

roughly on the floor of the holodeck, falling only a meter at most.

"Computer," the EMH said calmly. "Record session for review. Executive medical authorization: delta-sigma-Puccini." He offered Seven a hand up. "If I may?"

She sprang angrily to her feet, rejecting his overture. "What did you do?" she demanded.

"In my capacity as chief medical officer, I prescribed a few tweaks to your program . . . in your best interests, of course."

Her hand went instinctively to her throat, where the holographic tubules had seemingly jabbed her, but found only some slight residual soreness. The safety protocols had apparently been fully engaged after all.

"You violated our agreement."

"Not all," he insisted. "I never joined forces with you against the drone. I simply presented myself as a helpless victim . . . quite convincing, it seems."

"To what end?"

"Isn't that obvious? To provide you with a superior, more fundamentally human incentive to defeat the drone: to protect a friend."

Seven paused, grasping his intent. It occurred to her that, perhaps, she had never truly believed that she could overcome her earlier self, which was why she had always aborted the simulation once it became apparent that defeat was inevitable – until the battle was no longer just about her and her insecurities anymore.

"Yet the drone *did* succeed in injecting me with nanoprobes, if only fictionally. At best, we merely disabled each other."

The Doctor nodded. "But the point is, you didn't let that stop you this time. And that, just maybe, you should stop beating yourself up, metaphorically *and* holographically."

Seven contemplated her hand, recalling how it had ultimately sufficed to rip out the drone's eyepiece – once she was suitably motivated. She derived a significant degree of satisfaction from the memory.

"You have given me food for thought, Doctor. Thank you for your . . . prescription."

END ✦

Quality Of Life

STORY: CHRISTOPHER COOPER
ILLUSTRATION: LOUIE DE MARTINIS

A distant flash of lightning illuminated the façade of the old house. It was no castle, but imposed itself imperiously against the landscape nevertheless, perched as it was on the edge of a vertiginous clifftop. Its turrets, arches, and buttresses spoke of wealth and authority in a way that enthralled so many unimaginative beings of linear sentience. Q appreciated the ostentatiousness but was otherwise unimpressed.

The front door, however, did interest him. It was ancient, an antique far older than the house itself, with intricate motifs carved into its wooden panels relating a primeval tale of heroes and monsters. He smiled. Such histories, however mythologically represented, were always a matter of perspective, and it amused him that in this instance he knew the roles should have been reversed. After all, he had been partially responsible for the events depicted.

Q reached out and gripped the metal ring of the door's substantial iron knocker. He didn't have to knock to gain entry, of course, but he felt this majestic slab of craftmanship deserved a measure of respect. Rapping three times, he took a step back and waited.

* * *

The servant limped towards the door from the far side of the main hall. The joints in his prosthetic leg were playing up again. "I'm coming…" he wheezed, moving as best he could as another trio of impatient knocks rang out. "I'm coming!"

Hurriedly, he pulled back an assortment of rusty bolts before inserting a key and turning the lock with a clunk. Opening the heavy door just a crack, the old man peered out into the dusk, but there was no-one there. Perplexed, the servant opened it a little wider, straining to see along the single narrow pathway that meandered away from the house. There was no sign of anyone.

"You took your time," a voice echoed from inside the hall.

The servant span around, eyes wide. "How did you…?" he stuttered.

"I got bored of waiting so I thought I'd make myself at home," smiled Q, reclining in a leather armchair with a glass of wine in his hand, basking in the warmth of the hall's blazing hearth.

"Did you light that?" demanded the servant, taking several determined steps towards the visitor. "That's my job!"

Q sat forward. "Is it? And who might you be?"

"Bute," answered the man, puffing his chest out imperiously. "Augum Bute, the keeper of this house."

"And you are the only servant here?" Q asked, taking stock of the gaunt figure, clad in garments so tattered they'd give rags a bad name.

"I am no mere servant, Sir!" Bute bristled. With a start, he realized the stranger was suddenly standing right beside him.

"I can see that," murmured Q, examining Bute more closely. "More of a test bed. An ongoing experiment. A lab rat."

Q could see the evidence written all over Bute's face, quite literally. One of his deep-set eyes had been replaced with an array of miniature mechanical lenses, like the compound eye of an insect, while micro-scars wound their way along his left cheek and across his forehead, snaking towards a metallic plate fused into his skull. Strands of lank, grey hair partially obscured diodes welded roughly to the metal, an attempt by the man to disguise the addition.

"You're wrong," Bute objected. "The master looks after me. She helps me!" But Q could sense doubt had been festering in the man's mind for some time.

"I'm sure she does," Q assured him with mock sympathy. "Speaking of whom, I do believe it's time I introduced myself."

As Bute opened his mouth to protest, he found he was all alone.

*   *   *

The laboratory took up most of the upper floor of the house, where walls had been roughly knocked through to create a large, open space surrounded by a labyrinth of alcoves, filled with bookshelves overflowing with weighty tomes and scientific ephemera. Through a glazed section of roof, stars were beginning to flicker as night fell.

The scientist seemed oblivious to Q's arrival, her focus wholly consumed by a web of cables connecting a complex machine to a metal casket at the center of the lab. Q decided to observe her ministrations for a moment before announcing his presence. A surprise appearance always served to unsettle.

As she busied herself taking readings from a bank of monitoring devices, Doctor Maratheus presented the air of someone for whom their work was everything, to the exclusion of everything else. She was pale and thin, as if she'd forgotten to eat or sleep for days, but her eyes sparkled with each new positive result.

"I think this could be it." Bute, pass me the thiridium gauge," she barked excitedly at Q, evidently having mistaken the newcomer for her servant. Q picked up the nearest object and gave it to her.

"YOU'RE HERE FOR THE BIRTH OF SOMETHING SPECIAL." MARATHEUS BOASTED.

Maratheus glanced at the silver spoon in her hand and frowned. "What in…?"

She was interrupted by a crash as the laboratory door slammed open and Bute all but fell into the room, gulping for breath. "Master… stranger… here…" he gasped, pointing a shaking finger in Q's direction.

Bewildered, Maratheus looked first at her sweating, disheveled servant and then at Q. He flashed his most ingratiating smile at her in return.

"My dear doctor, I am at your service," he said, bowing politely. "Word of your experiments has reached the Centerium. You're making waves."

Maratheus blinked. "The Centerium? But… what do they know of my work?"

"Enough to send someone to peer review your discoveries."

"You?" she asked, tentatively.

Q smiled. The Centerium—the highest scientific authority on the planet—had no knowledge or interest in Maratheus' experiments, having disregarded her as a misguided crackpot decades ago. For his purposes, however, the implication that they had was enough to gain her confidence.

"They must have seen my pamphlet," Maratheus mused to herself with growing excitement. "This could mean funding. Sponsorship. Enough to employ a

proper assistant. A whole team!"

Wringing her hands with glee, she failed to notice Bute shifting uncomfortably at the very idea.

"Perhaps we could begin with an overview," suggested Q. "I'm intrigued."

"Of course, yes, absolutely!" Maratheus nodded enthusiastically. "Your timing is impeccable. Just before you arrived I made a breakthrough in neural mapping that should… *should*… finally solve the interface problem. You're here for the birth of something special!" she boasted.

"Now, isn't that a coincidence," said Q, raising a knowing eyebrow at Bute.

The servant frowned and waddled to his master's side. "How do we know he is who he says he is?" Bute whispered to her. "I don't trust him. He looks shifty."

"Do not embarrass me in front of our visitor," Maratheus hissed. "Get over there and reset the power convertors, or I'll have your other eye."

Bute bowed his head and skuttled away, throwing Q a spiteful glance.

"Where were we?" Maratheus paused to collect her thoughts. "Ah yes, an overview. What is your understanding of my research?"

"That you've made great advances in the field of bio-mechanical interoperability, namely a means of symbiotically linking organic beings with machines," Q replied. "I take it you've moved well beyond the results you achieved with this test case?"

It took a moment for Bute to realize the unwelcome visitor was talking about him. The servos in his prosthetic clenched involuntarily.

"One of my earliest successes," Maratheus stated proudly. "He's been invaluable to my work—my *life's* work! The fact he has survived this long has been a wonder. I'm not sure I would ever find another such malleable subject."

"Assistant," Bute interrupted. "I'm her assistant," he gulped, staring at Q defiantly.

"The convertors won't reset themselves, will they?" Maratheus

"THE BORG AREN'T ONES FOR HOME COMFORTS. GIVE THEM AN ALCOVE AND THEY SEEM HAPPY ENOUGH, NOT THAT THEY'RE ONES FOR HAPPINESS EITHER."

shot Bute an icy smile. He turned away sullenly, his eyes moist, and busied himself with his task. Q almost pitied him.

"What we really want to know is, what do you plan to do with this technology, should you succeed?"

"Isn't it obvious?" Maratheus replied, as if surprised that her goal should be in any doubt. "To allow my people to transcend the limits of the physical. To expand our perception of reality through the power of algorithms and emotions combined. I call it 'Hyper-sentience.' We would be unstoppable."

Q had heard enough. "That is precisely what concerns us. Let me show you something."

*　*　*

The sudden darkness was a shock, but the smell was something else entirely. Sterile yet charged with the tang of electrical current, it was like nothing Bute had smelt before. He blinked several times, anxiously hoping his eyes would adjust to the lack of light, and soon began to make out the shapes of Maratheus and that infernal visitor nearby.

"Master, where are we?" he asked. Clearly this wasn't the lab. They were in a corridor of sorts, although all Bute could see in the dim green light were pipes and conduits.

"I… I don't know," Maratheus shivered. "It's so cold."

"The Borg aren't ones for home comforts," Q told them. "Give them an alcove and they seem happy enough, not that they're ones for

happiness either."

"The… what? What is a 'Borg?'" Maratheus asked.

"The reason you're here, my dear," Q smiled and disappeared.

Bute and Maratheus glanced at each other, at a loss over what to do next. Then they heard the stranger's voice echo from the far end of the corridor, "This way."

"What is he…?" Bute uttered, dumbstruck.

"I don't know, but I'm beginning to think he has nothing to do with the Centerium," decided Maratheus.

They hurried after the stranger for several intersections until they encountered their first drone. The figure was part organic, heavily augmented with cybernetics, and appeared to be linked to a panel

of circuitry through a prosthetic interface where a hand might have been. Bute's leg had never felt more alien to him.

"I don't believe it," Maratheus smiled, approaching the drone in awe. "A bio-mechanoid. This is everything I've ever aspired to create. It's wonderful!"

Tentatively, she reached out to touch the drone. Laying her hand upon its shoulder, she felt… *nothing*. A complete absence of life. She snatched her hand away, horrified.

Its task completed, the drone detached itself, turned, and walked silently away. Maratheus watched it leave, entranced but left with an unexpected sense of uncertainty.

"Did you really think you were the first to explore the concept of such a combination?" asked Q.

"I had no idea I had competition in the field," she said. "Who invented these 'Borg'? Was it the Valatians? The Marsheen Republic? Surely not the Centerium itself?!"

"For a scientist with such grand vision, your imagination is sadly lacking," Q sneered. "The Borg have existed since before your ancestors laid waste to the only other intelligent species on your world."

Their location had changed again. They were still surrounded by the strange, dark metal architecture, but were now bathed in a raw, orange light. Bute whimpered in fear and clung onto Maratheus' arm, but she shrugged him away.

"What is this? A simulation?" Maratheus demanded. "You're clearly some kind of avatar."

"You seek to make your species 'unstoppable,'" Q challenged her. "Have you any idea what 'unstoppable' actually means? The Borg are the *definition* of unstoppable."

"But who are they?" Maratheus spat back.

"The inevitable outcome of a quest such as your own," Q said. "An insatiable hunger for knowledge that can never be sated, to the extent that

knowledge itself becomes meaningless. All they want is more, more, more, but the Borg have assimilated so many answers they've forgotten to keep asking themselves the only question that really matters: 'Why?'"

Bute was tugging at her sleeve, but Maratheus chose to ignore him.

"Are the answers you seek worth such a fate?" Q asked.

She replied without hesitation, defiant. "Yes. For the sake of my species' survival, yes they are."

"Master, look. Please!" Bute insisted. Maratheus turned impatiently towards him, then noticed the bright, orange object at which he was pointing. Through a gap in the expanse of black metal she could see a vast disc surrounded by stars. A planet. Her planet. And they were on a Borg spaceship moving towards it.

Maratheus turned to Q, her eyes wide. "They're coming to destroy us."

"No," Q reassured her. "They are going to assimilate you—your culture, your history, your dreams. Everything you've ever loved. Your species will achieve the immortality you seek, but it will have no meaning."

"Can't you stop it?"

"I could have. Why do you think I asked you that question?"

*   *   *

They were back in the lab, but the stranger wasn't with them.

Maratheus' mouth was dry. How long did they have? Was there time to send out a warning? Would anyone believe her, even if there was?

Her desperate thoughts were interrupted by the whine of the power convertors spooling. Startled, Maratheus looked towards her equipment. The systems hadn't been engaged before they'd been taken aboard the Borg spaceship. How could they be functioning now?

"Bute, shut the machine down," she ordered, but her servant didn't respond.

A hand gripped her upper arm, squeezing it like a vice. "Bute?" she cried out.

But his eyes were blank, his face expressionless.

"Resistance is futile."

END

A STAR TREK VOYAGER STORY

Retribution

STORY: LISA KLINK

J aneway's hometown had changed since the last time she was here. In the past twenty-two years, Bloomington, Indiana had become a hub of subspace research. The house she'd grown up in was now gone, and a sophisticated laboratory stood in its place. The celebratory parade for Janeway and her crew had passed right by the site on its way to the massive observatory where a reception was being held. It involved the usual speech making, this time by Bloomington's long-winded mayor, as well as a blizzard of hand shaking and congratulations from the local citizens.

"You're the reason I want to get into Starfleet Academy," a young woman told Janeway as they posed for a holo-picture together. "Your story really inspires me."

"That's kind of you to say." Janeway really was pleased to have impacted the woman's life, but after an hour of smiling and posing, she was growing weary of being the center of attention. One glance at Chakotay showed that he felt the same. She made her way over to him.

"Thank you for coming to this," she told him. "I can't believe the entire senior staff made it."

Chakotay smiled. "We all wanted to honor you." Starfleet had dropped all charges against him and the other former Maquis. He was going to lead his own crew now, as the captain of a diplomatic vessel, with Lieutenant Harry Kim as his first officer.

There were times when Janeway missed the excitement of space travel, but she found it very satisfying to train new captains at the Academy. She knew that Tuvok felt the same way as a security and tactical instructor on Vulcan, a position which allowed him to reconnect with his family. He'd come back to

Earth to help honor his captain and friend, gamely mingling with the enthusiastic spectators who had turned out for the event.

"No, I will not marry you." The calm declaration caught Janeway's attention, and she turned to see Seven of Nine facing a rather handsome Andorian. The young man seemed to handle the rejection well enough, settling for a holo-snapshot with his would-be fiancée. He gallantly kissed her on the hand, then rejoined the crowd of onlookers. Janeway couldn't help feeling proud of Seven, who was creating a meaningful life for herself as a member of the Federation's Borg Task Force. She was also pleased to see her protégé successfully navigating the social interactions required of her as a celebrated public figure.

Janeway approached her. "How many proposals is that now?"

"Two so far today. I'm still considering the one from the chief of police." Seven said it with a straight face, but Janeway knew her well enough to detect a joke. She smiled.

"Are you enjoying yourself at all?" asked Janeway.

"Not as much as the Doctor appears to be."

They looked up to see the Doctor pontificating in front of a rapt audience. He was positively enjoying his time in the spotlight, regaling his listeners with tales of derring-do. "Then we used an anesthetic gas to immobilize the Romulans on board and retook the ship," he told them, earning a few "ooh"s of appreciation. Janeway knew that the Doctor was less excited about being the subject of constant study by holographic engineers, but he tolerated their inquiries with minimal disdain.

After leaving Miral with a babysitter, Tom and B'Elanna had arrived in the *Delta Flyer*, which was currently parked in geosynchronous orbit. On Janeway's recommendation, Starfleet had gifted them the ship after their return to Earth. The couple looked happy, she thought, a far cry from the troubled pilot and engineer she'd first met on the other side of the galaxy. Now B'Elanna was designing experimental ships and Tom was test flying them. Janeway was about to go talk to them, when Seven suddenly clutched her arm.

"Captain…" she started to say, swaying on her feet. Then she dropped to the ground and began to convulse.

Chakotay swiftly knelt beside her. "Seven!"

The Doctor was already hurrying over to help. He cushioned Seven's head as she shook. "I need an emergency kit," he called, as the skin around the implant over her eye began to turn an angry red.

The Mayor quickly sent his aide to retrieve an emergency kit from the park's community center and brought it to him. The Doctor removed a hypospray and injected her. Seven's convulsions eased, then stopped, leaving her unconscious.

He took out the medical tricorder and scanned her with it. "There's some kind of neurolytic pathogen affecting her Borg implants. It's killing the surrounding tissue."

"A pathogen? Where did it come from?" Janeway wondered.

"That's a good question," said the Doctor. "Based on its spread, it was introduced into her body via the implants in her left hand. It only would have taken a touch."

Janeway looked at the dozens of people around them. "Whoever did it could still be here."

Tuvok turned to the security guard monitoring the event. "Seal off the exits."

The guard quickly pressed several buttons on his PADD. The two doors leading out of the observatory sealed shut, prompting a murmur of alarm from the crowd.

"Can you counteract this pathogen?" asked B'Elanna.

The Doctor looked at the readings on his tricorder and shook his head. "It's actively evolving to fight her body's defenses. Even if I

get her to a medical facility, I'd need a sample of the original strain to develop a treatment."

"We've got to find out who's responsible," said Janeway. "They may still have some of the original strain."

The Doctor checked his tricorder. "I'm detecting some trace skin cells left on her implants. They're Andorian."

"The marriage proposal," Janeway remembered. She scanned the crowd for the Andorian, and saw him standing calmly among the onlookers. "You. Don't move."

Tuvok quickly moved in and restrained the alien, who made no attempt to escape. He kept his eyes fixed on Seven. "I want you to tell your Borg friend that she's dying at the hands of Sirkan, father of three children assimilated by the Collective."

"Seven wasn't responsible for that," Janeway objected.

"They're all responsible. And I intend to use this pathogen on every single drone." He activated his subdermal communicator. "Sirkan to the *Acheron*, one to beam up." Then he dematerialized, vanishing from Tuvok's grip.

Janeway hit her combadge. "This is Captain Janeway calling

Earth Monitoring Station. Is there a ship called the *Acheron* currently in orbit?"

The answer came swiftly. "They're just breaking orbit, at full impulse."

Janeway's first instinct was to beam up to *Voyager* and give chase, but her ship was currently being analyzed and repaired at the Utopia Planetia shipyard. She turned to Tom, but he anticipated her request. "We can catch them in the *Delta Flyer*," he said.

Janeway turned to the Doctor. "Get Seven to Starfleet Medical."

"I'm going with them," Chakotay insisted.

She nodded. "The rest of us will go in the *Flyer* and catch up to Sirkan. We'll get you a sample of the original pathogen as soon as we can."

"Please hurry," said the Doctor. "She doesn't have much time before her organs begin to shut down."

Janeway joined Tom, B'Elanna, Tuvok and Harry. Tom tapped his combadge. "Paris to *Delta Flyer*. Five to beam up."

The onboard computer transported the group up to the *Flyer*. Tom went to the helm while B'Elanna checked sensors.

TOM MATCHED THE OTHER SHIP'S COURSE AND SPEED AS SIRKAN HEADED TOWARD MARS, THEN ZIPPED AROUND IT...

"I'm picking up the *Acheron*'s ion trail, bearing 233.5," she announced.

"Pursuit course. Full impulse," said Janeway.

Tom nodded. "Yes, ma'am."

The *Delta Flyer* sped off after the fleeing ship. "It's fifty thousand kilometers ahead of us," B'Elanna reported.

"Hail Sirkan," said Janeway.

Harry sent out a hail. "No response."

She looked to Tuvok at the tactical station. "As soon as we're within weapons range, take out his engines. But don't cause too much damage. We need to get on board and find that pathogen."

"Forty thousand kilometers…"

"Firing phasers," said Tuvok.

But as he did, the *Acheron* made evasive maneuvers, and the phaser blast barely glanced off the port nacelle.

"You think you can get away that easy?" Tom matched the other ship's course and speed as Sirkan headed toward Mars, then zipped around it and continued toward deep space.

Tuvok fired again. This time the blast struck near the warp core. "Their warp drive is off line. Shields down to 80 percent."

Janeway turned to Harry. "Look for any vulnerability that allows us to beam aboard that ship."

"On it. But we need to get closer."

Tom smiled. "Consider it done."

As they approached Jupiter, the *Acheron* flew around one of the planet's outermost moons. The *Flyer* did the same, pursuing the other ship as it ducked in and out among Jupiter's seventy-nine satellites, skimming the surface of Lysithia and ricocheting off the thin atmosphere of Europa.

"We're closing on them, Captain," said Harry.

Janeway told Tuvok, "Hit their shields again."

But before he could fire, the *Acheron* abruptly dove toward Jupiter and plunged into the gaseous atmosphere. The *Flyer* followed. But it was impossible to see through the thick gasses.

"Do you have him on sensors?" asked Tom.

B'Elanna pressed a few controls. "I can detect the plasma discharge from their engines."

A new image appeared on the front screen of the *Delta Flyer*, showing the *Acheron* in bright red amid the swirling yellow and green gasses. It careened from side to side, up and down, trying to shake the pursuing vessel, but Tom matched every move.

Tuvok fired phasers, striking the *Acheron*'s shield generators. "Shields at forty percent."

"Can we transport on board?" asked Janeway.

Harry checked his readings. "Not yet. One more hit ought to do it."

But then the *Acheron* emerged from Jupiter's atmosphere, heading directly for Ganymede, its largest moon. As the *Flyer* approached, Sirkan veered off to take cover behind the massive satellite. Tom pursued him, but Sirkan managed to keep Ganymede between the two ships. Tuvok no longer had a shot.

Tom shook his head in frustration. "We'll never catch them like this."

"And Seven's running out of time." Janeway hit her combadge. "This is Janeway to Starfleet Command. We could use a couple more ships out here by Jupiter to pursue a fugitive."

An official sounding voice came over the com. "I can have a cargo ship rendezvous with you within the hour."

"That's too long."

B'Elanna was startled by something on her monitor. "Captain, I'm picking up another vessel on approach."

A medical transport ship appeared from behind the moon Callisto. Chakotay's voice came over the com. "Need a hand?"

Janeway smiled. "Chakotay. I thought you were staying with Seven."

JANEWAY GRABBED A PHASER FROM THE *DELTA FLYER*'S CACHE OF WEAPONS...

"Thought I could do her more good out here. The head of Starfleet Medical was kind enough to lend me a ship."

"Do you have any weapons?"

"No. But your fugitive doesn't know that," he said. "I'll cut him off."

Chakotay headed for the *Acheron*. The other ship tried to retreat, only to find the *Delta Flyer* closing in from its port side. The *Flyer* discharged another phaser blast, striking the *Acheron*'s shield generator.

"His shields are down," Tuvok reported.

"We're close enough to transport, Captain," said Harry.

"Prepare to transport," she told him, then nodded to Tuvok. "You're with me."

Janeway grabbed a phaser from the *Flyer*'s cache of weapons and went to stand on the transporter pad. Tuvok got his own weapon and followed.

She nodded to Harry. "Energize." He activated the transporter and the two of them dematerialized.

They found themselves on the bridge of the *Acheron*, a small science vessel overstuffed with laboratory equipment. The rounded walls were coated with bioluminescent gel that provided a greenish glow. It was like being inside the belly of an enormous beast.

Sirkan turned from the ship's controls to find Janeway and Tuvok holding phasers on him. "We don't want to hurt you," she said, controlling her anger. "We want a sample of the neurolytic pathogen you used on Seven to make an antidote."

Sirkan faced them, unafraid. "I'm not doing anything to help *her*. I'd sooner destroy it than give it to you."

Janeway indicated the mess of equipment. "Search the lab." As Tuvok began to look through the clusters of machinery, she turned back to Sirkan. "I'm sorry to hear about your children. But Seven was as much a victim of the Borg as they

were. She was only a child herself when she was assimilated."

The Andorian was unmoved. "I don't care how or when she was assimilated, only that she was part of the Collective. She still is, as far as I'm concerned. And they all deserve to die."

"Even your own children?" she asked.

"They would thank me for destroying them now."

Janeway saw his eyes flick, very briefly, toward a cabinet built into the wall of the laboratory. "Check that cabinet," she told Tuvok.

"No!" shouted Sirkan as he dove for his own weapon, concealed beneath a console. As he brought the weapon up to fire, Janeway stunned him with her phaser. Sirkan collapsed.

Tuvok opened the cabinet to find several vials of clear liquid. "Collect every sample you can find," said Janeway. "Then let's get back to the *Flyer*."

They beamed back to the *Delta Flyer* and ran preliminary scans of the substance in the vials. It matched the chemical makeup that the Doctor had identified in the pathogen.

Janeway returned to the captain's chair. Maybe she did miss being in command of a starship more than she'd thought. With great satisfaction, she issued the order, "Mr. Paris, set a course for Earth."

She and Chakotay were by Seven's bedside when she regained consciousness. "What happened?" she asked them. "Am I ill?"

"You were poisoned," said Chakotay.

"By whom?" Seven inquired.

Janeway spoke gently to her friend. "It doesn't matter now. He was misguided."

Seven looked up at her. "Why do I suspect that I have you to thank for my recovery?"

"Everyone worked together. You have to know how much you mean to all of us," Janeway assured her.

"Please express my appreciation to the rest of the crew."

The captain smiled. "You can tell them yourself. We have another reception at Starfleet Headquarters next week."

While Chakotay gave a mild groan, Seven returned Janeway's smile. "I will look forward to that." ✦

A *STAR TREK: THE NEXT GENERATION* STORY

Broken Oaths

STORY: CHRIS DOWS

"For the last time Doctor Zimmerman, will you *please* stop interrupting other members of the clinical taskforce while they are speaking?"

Beverly Crusher looked to Doctor Chang in bewilderment. As Chair of this specially assembled meeting in Starfleet Medical's imposing conference room, the diminutive figure had tried to keep things civil, but Beverly could see her usual good humour had been ground down by Zimmerman's relentless interjections over the last four hours. And it hadn't just been Beverly who'd suffered his disrespect – every one of her half-dozen fellow physicians and Vice-Admiral Blackwell, who Beverly knew as an acquaintance of Jean-Luc's, had been treated with equal disdain. Several attempts to start her presentation had been objected to or dismissed with a wave of a hand by the insufferable man sitting opposite, with this last agenda item, the one Beverly had travelled halfway across the Alpha Quadrant to debate in person, seemingly causing the mighty director of the EMH programme the greatest concern.

"Technically, Doctor Crusher is *not* a member of the taskforce. Other than voicing her objections to my work over the last year, she has had no part in the development of the Emergency Medical Hologram programme – for which I am eternally grateful."

Doctor Chang stared at Zimmerman for long seconds. Beverly could see she was holding her PADD so tightly, her knuckles had gone white. Struggling to keep her own emotions and hypertension under control, Beverly folded her arms and concentrated on her breathing.

"Doctor Crusher is here in recognition of the significant role she has played in gathering information on the greatest threat Starfleet has ever faced. I strongly suggest you extend her that courtesy."

Zimmerman closed his eyes at Chang's words and shrugged. Taking that as a reluctant acknowledgement, Chang turned to the taskforce sitting around the huge oval table and spoke with forced calm.

"If you would all please refer to the information designated 'Borg Dataset zero four zero' on your PADDs, I will invite Doctor Crusher to continue."

Beverly nodded to Chang in response and got to her feet as the group looked to their devices. Their expressions ranged from annoyance to impatience, and Beverly reminded herself not everyone dressed in blue shared her opinion. Zimmerman folded his arms and sighed theatrically.

"Fellow taskforce members, I would again like thank you for this opportunity to speak today. I appreciate my perspective on this matter may appear controversial, contradictory to my role as a physician even, but as the person responsible for the great majority of the information contained in this dataset, I feel it is my moral duty to – "

"Your moral duty? What about your duty of care?"

Beverly raised her eyebrows at Zimmerman, who stared back, unblinking, with coal-black eyes. Out of the corner of her eye, Beverly saw Chang's jaw set firm. She was clearly very tired of being undermined.

"Doctor Zimmerman, you've already made it clear you'd rather be back in your laboratories on Jupiter Station than continue with this meeting which, despite its importance to Starfleet Medical and the Fleet, you consider to be little more than a trivial distraction. The more you interrupt, the longer it will take for you to return."

Zimmerman opened his mouth to spit out an undoubtedly sarcastic retort but to Beverly's surprise, he immediately closed it without speaking. Beverly pressed on.

"As I was saying, I feel it is my moral duty to request Borg Dataset zero four zero is not incorporated into the EMH database."

Even though the taskforce knew her request was coming, Beverly stating it out loud created quite the impact – particularly with Zimmerman, who shook his head vehemently. Retaking her seat, she felt her heart beating in her chest, adrenaline pumping through her body in a classic fight or flight response. She just had to ensure she didn't lose her temper with that intolerable man and, with it, her argument.

Doctor Chang waited for murmured conversations between the group to die down, then addressed the room.

"Who would like to open the debate?"

Vice-Admiral Blackwell cleared her throat.

"May I ask why you feel this is a question of morality, Doctor Crusher? I'm struggling to see any great ethical dilemma here. I'm not medically trained I'll grant you that, but surely this is a resource that could be of considerable benefit to the EMH project?"

"At last. Some sense from Starfleet."

Beverly was impressed that Blackwell didn't show a flicker of acknowledgement to Zimmerman's comment. It was the question she had hoped to hear, the one she had travelled all this way to answer. Ignoring Zimmerman's barb, she continued.

"I have encountered the collective several times. While the first meeting provided limited medical information, during the rescue and

BEVERLY KNEW HER VOICE WAS GETTING LOUDER. ZIMMERMAN NARROWED HIS EYES...

subsequent convalescence of Captain Picard, we were able to briefly access the Borg's enormous assimilation database. More significantly, my work with the former drone Hugh gave me the opportunity to further study Borg anatomy and to enhance our understanding of their physiology. While I entirely agree information on Borg assimilation should be included in the EMH programme, the rest of the data – specifically that taken from the collective's own archives – is, in my opinion, a chronicle of violations on unwilling, terrified victims."

She knew she was skirting dangerously close to the dramatic in her choice of language, but it best conveyed how serious Beverly felt the issue to be.

"Very colourful turn of phrase, Doctor. Perhaps you should resign your commission and take up writing holo-novels instead."

Beverly crossed her arms and tapped her fingers lightly on her arms.

After months of unspoken animosity between the two, she shook her head lightly at Chang's unspoken offer of chastisement and braced herself for the verbal assault she knew had been building up for months prior to this ill-tempered meeting.

"Your problem, and by 'your' I mean everybody except me in this room, is that you're assigning an ethical dimension to something that doesn't need it. Data is data, regardless of how it is achieved. Its value is a binary state – either useful and therefore included, or useless and discarded."

"I think you would be well-served, as the self-appointed template for your creation, to look at things from a more humane and compassionate perspective Doctor Zimmerman. I shudder to think what kind of bedside manner your 'holo-doctor' is going to have."

Beverly deliberately emphasised the epithet, knowing full well it had been discounted early in the meeting

– much to Zimmerman's annoyance and a few wry smiles from her fellow practitioners. Zimmerman's brow furrowed, clearly wounded by the reminder.

"There is no function for compassion in the decision-making progress. Resistance to the logic of its use is, to coin a phrase, futile."

There was a sharp intake of breath from a couple of the taskforce at Zimmerman's deliberately provocative statement. Beverly felt her jaw ache with the pressure of keeping her mouth shut. His dismissive air was one thing, but to incorporate the words of a soulless, relentless enemy bent on the destruction of everything Beverly held dear was unconscionable. Inevitably, Zimmerman continued.

"You've already admitted any medical information relating to the Borg is important, so why hold back on using all of what's available because of some fanciful notion the universe will be a happier place if you don't? It won't. No one will care, other than the poor unfortunate who's just had tubules stuck into their neck and must be executed by their crewmates because a potentially critical piece of information on their species' reaction to the process hadn't been included."

Zimmerman was on his feet now, hands resting in his open lab-coat pockets. Why he felt he had to wear that, Beverly had no idea. Slowly, she unfolded her arms and pushed herself to her feet, matching his eye level with hands flat on the polished table surface.

"The information was gathered through pain and suffering, Doctor Zimmerman. The only binary state I can see here is whether we add to the abuse these victims endured or not by choosing to use this unethically collected data."

Beverly knew her voice was getting louder. Zimmerman narrowed his eyes and stroked his chin.

"Tell me Doctor Crusher, just how 'ethical' was it for you to rescue that Borg drone in the first place, against the express wishes of your Captain, then go on record as objecting to the development of a weapon that could have destroyed the entire collective had it been deployed?"

Beverly felt her stomach drop. This was a low blow, and while Jean-Luc had wisely decided to allow Hugh's return to the Collective in the hope – correct, as it turned out – his new-found free will would be just as effective as a virus, her actions had been questioned on more than one occasion. Even as she replied, she knew she was on shaky ground.

"I don't see how that is pertinent to this debate."

Zimmerman raised his eyebrows in mock shock.

"Oh really? Let me make it pertinent. Your previous moral stand might have led to the death of billions then. Your current moral stand may lead to the death of thousands in the future. I, for one, am not going to allow it – and neither should any of you."

Zimmerman looked to each doctor in turn, then back to Beverly before continuing.

"I think you've all forgotten something. 'I swear this oath by Apollo physician, by Aesculapius, by Health, and by all the gods and goddesses: In whatsoever place that I enter I will enter to help the sick and heal the injured, and I will do no harm'."

Beverly stared at Zimmerman in astonishment. She couldn't believe he would dare quote the Hippocratic Oath to justify his argument. What of the harm that had been done to obtain this terrible data? No sick had been helped then, nor any injured healed. It was as inappropriate as it was insulting. Beverly looked to Chang, who was clearly struggling to control her own anger, then to the others. Blackwell looked bemused, while Beverly's fellow doctors either shook their heads or glowered at Zimmerman. Even his staunchest allies in the medical community would find *that* hard to accept. The room fell into a dark silence, and just as Beverly was about to reply, the exterior doors hissed open.

A hunched figure shuffled into the room. Arms behind his back, he regarded the taskforce with piercing blue eyes then made his unhurried way to an empty chair. Easing himself down with a grunt, Beverly looked to Chang, who was clearly astonished at the man's unexpected appearance. Everyone was.

"Well now doctors. Seems we have ourselves a sticky situation here."

Chang began to speak, but the old man waved her down.

"I've been following this project for some time now. Pretty impressive."

Zimmerman smirked, taking the compliment from the new arrival as further acknowledgement of his brilliance. However, Beverly could see there was more to come in the old man's deeply wrinkled face.

"Thing is, questions always need to be asked about anything new, and you were right to ask 'em young lady. I've done the same in my time but even this old country doctor can learn new tricks – did y'all get that medical procedure I sent you?"

Zimmerman nodded to the white-haired old man's question.

"Y'all remember the Genesis device? I told everyone who'd listen it was immoral and unethical, but then it ended up saving the life – hell, giving back the life – of someone very close to me."

Everyone hung on to the man's gently drawled words.

"Now I'm not saying you should ride roughshod over people's opinions just because you disagree with 'em. That's just poor manners. But if you listened to folk as much as you talked boy, you might be surprised how useful it can be."

The old man stared pointedly at Zimmerman, who stared back defiantly. Beverly could see anger rising in the scientist's face.

"That's all well and good, but empty platitudes and a few folksy homilies are unlikely to resolve this situation, Doctor McCoy."

The room erupted at Zimmerman's astonishing lack of respect shown to the retired Chief of Starfleet Medical. Chang tried her best to regain control, but it took McCoy rising shakily to his feet for the room to eventually come to order. Beverly could see the twinkle in his eye had gone, replaced by something much colder and sharper.

"You know who you remind me of, Doctor? Richard Daystrom. He was arrogant, self-opinionated, and convinced he was always the

"NONE OF YOU HERE HAVE BEEN AS INVOLVED WITH THE BORG AS I, AND I HOPE YOU NEVER WILL."

cleverest fella in the room. And what did that lead to? M-5. And that damned thing caused some real problems, if I recall."

As Zimmerman gaped at the comparison, Beverly took it as a cue to retaliate.

"That's the point I've been trying to make for months. His EMH cannot – "

"Woah there, young lady. I hadn't finished speaking. Now, with the involvement of others at his institute, what came from Daystrom's work eventually benefitted everybody. It just took a little bit of… objectivity."

McCoy's eyes burned into Beverly's.

"Call me an old fool, but I can see a time, not too far from now perhaps, where a ship might be far from home, lose its doctor, and its crew be totally reliant for its very survival on the EMH. In those circumstances, they'd need *every* scrap of medical information they could get their hands on. For that to happen, to misquote a pointy-eared friend of mine, the needs of the many must outweigh the misgivings of the few."

With that, the old man grunted, turned and made his leisurely way out of the room.

"Doctor Crusher… I believe you were speaking."

Beverly acknowledged Doctor Chang's softly spoken prompt, then turned to Zimmerman. He looked stunned, the Starfleet legend's comparison with Daystrom having clearly struck home. As Beverly thought through McCoy's words, something occurred to her. She'd spent so much time building animosity against Zimmerman the man she'd confused it with Zimmerman the scientist, someone who, with the EMH programme, was trying to do the right thing the wrong way – from her perspective at least.

"None of you here have been involved with the Borg as I, and I pray you never will. While I remain unconvinced of the moral perspective, I can see the benefits of including this information in the EMH database. Therefore, I withdraw my request for its removal."

Zimmerman tried not to smile too broadly but failed, and with sighs of gratefulness Chang declared the meeting over and the group hastily grabbed their PADDs and left, Zimmerman leading the rapid exodus. This left Beverly with Doctor Chang, who regarded her with a look of relief.

"Are you okay with this Beverly?"

Beverly smiled as she gathered up her own belongings.

"It's like McCoy said – at some point, the EMH might indeed meet the needs of the many. But here's an oath I'll swear to now. I'll never use the damned thing." ⬆

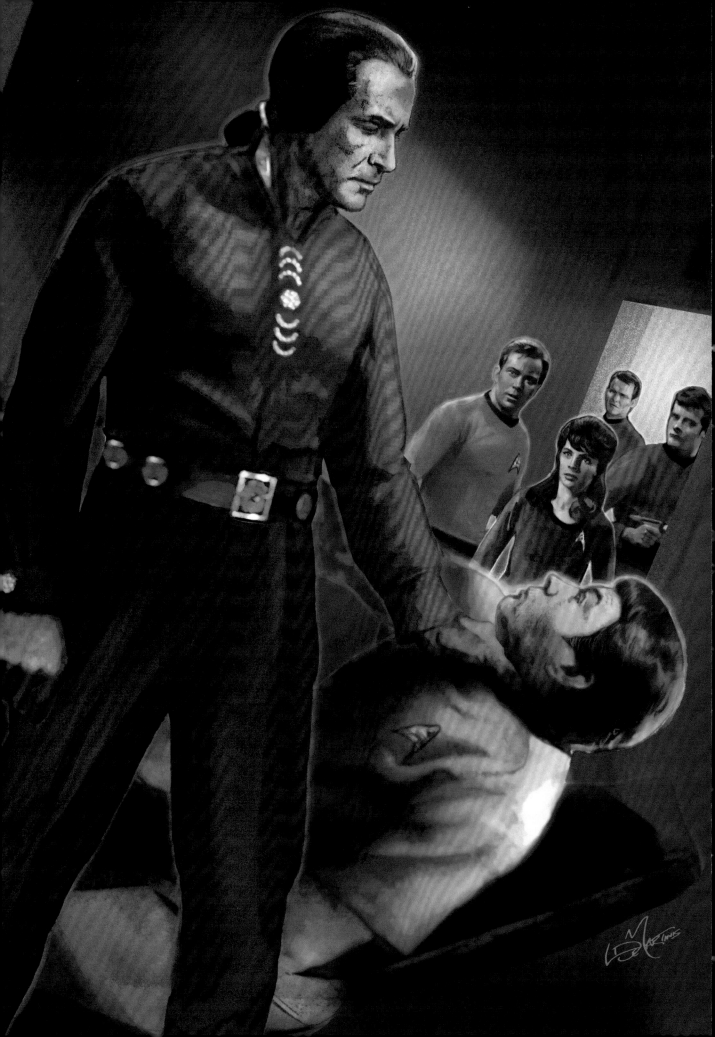

A *STAR TREK* STORY

The Way To Exile

STORY: GREG COX
ILLUSTRATION: LOUIE DE MARTINIS

"He's asking to see you, Captain."

"Very well." Kirk replied via the intercom on his armrest. "I'm on my way." He rose from the captain's chair and headed for the turbolift. "Mister Spock, you have the bridge."

The turbolift brought him quickly to the ship's brig, where Khan Noonien Singh waited behind a force field set to maximum strength. The one-time ruler of more than quarter of Earth's population, now clad in a plain red jumpsuit, was enjoying a monitored visit with Lieutenant Marla McGivers, the disgraced Starfleet officer who had elected to follow Khan into exile following his short-lived takeover of the *Enterprise*. They both looked up as Kirk approached.

"Ah, Captain," Khan said grandly, as though welcoming a guest rather greeting his jailor. He rose from the bench he had been sitting on with McGivers. "How good of you to join us."

"Khan," Kirk acknowledged him tersely. He nodded at a pair of stone-faced security officers, who drew their type-2 phaser pistols before deactivating the force field long enough for McGivers to exit the cell. A third officer waited to escort McGivers back to her quarters, where she was currently confined until the *Enterprise* reached its destination: an uninhabited planet in the Ceti Alpha system.

"Captain," she said, their encounters still awkward after her betrayal. "Thank you again for allowing me to record Khan's memories of 20th-century Earth for posterity. Makes me feel like I'm still the ship's historian, for the time being."

"You're welcome, Lieutenant." He did her the courtesy of using her rank, although it could be argued she'd lost that privilege after throwing her lot in with Khan and his fellow Augments; that term, Kirk had learned, was what genetically-engineered superhumans like Khan had once been called. "No doubt Federation scholars will find these interviews of value, even allowing for Khan's arguably skewed perspective."

She glanced at the looming security officers. "I don't suppose Khan and I could have a bit more . . . privacy?"

Kirk shook his head. He couldn't risk allowing Khan and McGivers to conspire unobserved. "You'll have privacy enough when we arrive at Ceti Alpha V, assuming you still intend to accompany Khan and his party there."

"I've made up my mind, Captain."

She departed with her escort and Kirk stepped up to the edge of Khan's cell. Only the invisible force field separated him from the vanquished conqueror, who had already demonstrated that locked doors were not enough to contain him.

"You asked to see me?" Kirk said, all business.

"It is about my people. I should like to visit them in person, to check on their condition and perhaps rally their spirits. As a leader, you surely appreciate the importance of maintaining morale."

At present, Khan's followers were confined to a force-shielded cargo bay temporarily repurposed to serve as a secure holding facility large enough to house seventy-plus survivors of Earth's long-ago Eugenics Wars. Forty-two men and thirty women, to be exact.

"The last time you rallied your troops," Kirk reminded Khan, "you took over my ship and nearly killed me. You'll forgive me if I'm not in a hurry to let you incite another insurrection."

For better or for worse, Ceti Alpha V lay in a remote sector of space, far off the beaten path of any known starfaring civilizations, so the *Enterprise* was still days away from dropping off Khan and his confederates. In theory, the planet's extreme isolation would protect the rest of the galaxy from Khan's ambitions, but in the meantime Kirk still had dozens of disgruntled Augments on his hands, along with their imperious leader.

"I see." Khan frowned. "If not in person then, perhaps via a closed-circuit monitor?"

"Sorry. Your people are being well cared for, I assure you, but they're going to have to do without your leadership for the duration." Kirk stepped away from the cell. "If there's anything else?"

"No, Captain. You've made your position quite clear."

Energy flared and crackled as Khan tested the force field with his fingertips. The guards tensed, drawing their sidearms once more, but the field held and Khan withdrew to his cot, where he resumed reading a hardcover edition of *Paradise Lost.* Kirk got the distinct impression he was being dismissed.

He turned his back on Khan, not without a certain uneasiness.

The sooner they reached Ceti Alpha V, the better.

* * *

"Are we sure this so-called medical emergency is for real?" Doctor McCoy asked as he was led into the makeshift prison in the cargo bay, accompanied by a full complement of armed security personnel. "I wasn't born yesterday, you know."

"Me either." Lieutenant Commander Giotto watched intently as his security team herded the captive Augments over to the far side of the spacious compartment, away from their supposedly stricken comrade. "But what do I know about diagnosing three-hundred-year-old super-people from the past?"

He had a point, McCoy conceded. Physicals conducted in the wake of the Augments' defeat had indicated that they were all in good health – exceptionally so, in fact. Then again, they had all just spent centuries in suspended animation. Who knew what delayed reactions they might experience?

Moving as briskly as caution allowed, McCoy and his bodyguards navigated orderly rows of cots, tables, and other furnishings to reach a male

him over."

According to Giotto, a guard had already prudently handcuffed the patient's hands together. Drawing nearer, McCoy recognized the seemingly unconscious figure as Joaquin, Khan's brutal henchman, who had once slapped Uhura when she'd refused to take orders from Khan. Lingering outrage on her behalf tested McCoy's Hippocratic Oath, but a doctor couldn't always choose his patients. He shoved his personal feelings toward the man aside to pass a handheld medical scanner over the Augment's hefty form. The device whirred mechanically.

"Hmm. I'm not detecting any obvious causes for concern. How long has he been--?"

"For Khan!"

Without warning, Ling took a running leap that sent her hurling over the recumbent patient toward McCoy's bodyguards. Sizzling phaser beams stunned her in mid-air but sheer momentum carried

"THE LAST TIME YOU RALLIED YOUR TROOPS," KIRK REMINDED KHAN, "YOU TOOK OVER MY SHIP AND NEARLY KILLED ME."

Augment lying motionless on a cot beneath a reflective thermal blanket. A solitary woman – Ling, McCoy believed her name was –watched anxiously over the man.

"He kept saying he was cold, that he felt like he was freezing. I told him to take a nap . . . and now we can't wake him up!"

McCoy exchanged a worried look with Giotto. Was this indeed a result of the man's long hibernation aboard the *Botany Bay*?

"Back away from him, please," the security officer instructed. "Let the doctor look

her into the security team, momentarily disrupting their watch over McCoy.

"What the..?" the doctor blurted.

Joaquin's eyes snapped open. With breathtaking speed and strength, he took advantage of the distraction to break his restraints and throw aside the blanket. A powerful hand gripped McCoy's throat before the doctor – or his guards – even realized what was happening.

"Nobody move!" Joaquin growled. "Or I'll crush his neck in a heartbeat!"

He wasn't exaggerating, McCoy knew. The scanner clattered to the floor as McCoy tried in vain to pry steel-like fingers away from his throat. He might have just as well have attempted to break free of a magnetic vise.

Damn it, he thought. *I was afraid of this.*

"Let him go!" Giotto demanded, moments too late. A half-dozen phasers suddenly targeted Joaquin, while additional officers tensely watched the other Augments in case they tried to rush the outnumbered security team. "Release him at once."

Could the phasers stun Joaquin fast enough to stop him from killing his hostage in an instant? Would the Augment's fist crush McCoy's cervical vertebrae the minute a beam jolted his nervous system? McCoy had to assume Giotto was asking himself those questions right now – and maybe not liking the answers.

"Lower your weapons." Joaquin glowered at Giotto, ignoring the officer's commands. Keeping a tight grip on McCoy's neck, the beefy Augment rose to his feet, using the doctor as a human shield. "And no tricks this time. One whiff of knock-out gas and your doctor is a corpse."

Déjà vu afflicted McCoy as he recalled Khan holding a knife to his throat not too long ago.

"What is it with you people and threatening your doctors?" he croaked, despite the alarming pressure on his throat. "Superior beings my foot!"

"Quiet." Joaquin squeezed tighter. "I'm doing the talking now."

Giotto held his fire. "What do you want?"

"Khan. And then this ship."

* * *

"I need you to tell your people to stand down," Kirk told Khan. "For everyone's sake."

"I see. So *now* you will permit me to communicate with them." Khan smiled coldly from the other side of the force field, clearly relishing the changed dynamic. "When it is *your* people who require deliverance."

Less than an hour had passed since McCoy had been taken hostage. A tense stand-off was underway; despite his

threats, Joaquin couldn't immediately kill McCoy without losing his only bargaining chip, but the volatile situation grew more dangerous with each passing moment. Kirk needed to end this before Joaquin and the other Augments ran out of patience.

"Please, Khan," McGivers urged him. "Don't let them hurt Doctor McCoy. Stop this before it's too late."

Including her in this negotiation was a calculated risk, given her divided loyalties, but she had intervened to save Kirk's own life before, when Khan had seized control of the ship. If there was even a chance she could appeal to the better angels of Khan's nature, Kirk needed to take that risk. McCoy's life might depend on it.

"The doctor is a brave man, worthy of respect." A rueful tone entered Khan's voice. "I regret that he's been placed in jeopardy, but sometimes hard sacrifices must be made to achieve a greater purpose. My first loyalty is to my own people – and our ultimate triumph." He sneered at Kirk. "Why settle for a world when we can have a galaxy?"

Was Khan once more aspiring to capture the *Enterprise*? Kirk realized he needed to squash that notion in no uncertain terms.

"Listen up, Khan. I don't know how you think this is going to end, but let me be clear: I will *never* surrender the *Enterprise* to you, even if, as you say, I have to sacrifice McCoy. And understand this, too: If your followers kill any of my crew, I will be forced to open the cargo bay doors and flush them all out into

space . . . for the safety of my ship."

McGivers gasped, but Khan merely chuckled.

"You're bluffing, Kirk."

"Not where the security of my ship is concerned." Kirk met Khan's gaze unflinchingly. "You're a leader, too. What would you do in my case?"

Khan scowled, and was that a trace of uncertainty in his eyes?

"You're not me, Kirk. Far from it."

"That's right. You're the famous Khan Noonien Singh." Kirk appealed to the other man's sense of pride and honor. "The Khan in the history books didn't spill blood for no reason, out of spite and revenge. In the end, he did what was best for his people, leading them out into space in search of a fresh start on a new world. He didn't throw away their best chance at a better future just to go down fighting instead."

"Please, Khan, hear what he's saying," McGivers entreated. "Ceti Alpha V is waiting for us. We can have a life there, just like we've talked about. You can conquer a world, forge an empire, found a dynasty. Isn't that better than some pointless conflict that can only get people hurt and killed . . . on both sides?"

Kirk prayed they were getting through to him, but feared Khan's mercurial temperament would get the better of him. Khan had, after all, attempted to blow up the *Enterprise*, killing everyone aboard, including his own people, the last time he'd faced defeat. What if he again preferred a pyrrhic victory to surrender?

"Think of your people, Khan. Put

them before your pride."

"My people have struck back in my name, Kirk. They're counting on me to seize the advantage they've so boldly provided me. Shall I now disappoint them?" He shook his head, perhaps a trifle reluctantly. "Capitulation is not in our nature."

"Neither is folly," Kirk argued. "Use your superior intellect, Khan. Your people are counting on you, yes, to chart the best course for them, just like you did three centuries ago when you dared to lead them to the stars. Be that man again, Khan. That leader. Choose hope over vengeance."

"And be the man I love, Khan," McGivers said. "The one I want to spend the rest of my life with. I believe in you, Khan. I know you'll do the right thing, for all of us."

Khan fell silent for a moment, his gaze shifting from Kirk to McGivers and back again. For a moment, Kirk worried that Khan's monumental ego was impervious to their words, but then he took a deep breath and stepped back from the force field.

"So be it. Let me speak to my people, as their commander."

"All right," Kirk said, all too aware that he was taking yet another risk. It was always possible that, despite his seeming change of heart, Khan would double-cross him by inflaming his people rather than calming them. Could he truly trust Khan this far? He questioned McGivers with his eyes. She nodded quietly, confirming his gut sense that Khan was on the level. Assuming he could trust her as well . . . .

Kirk crossed the brig to the nearest intercom panel. "Kirk to Uhura. I'm putting Khan on. Pipe his transmission to the Augments in the cargo bay via the public-address system. Let them all hear him."

"Aye, sir," Uhura answered from the bridge. "You're good to go."

Kirk kept his finger on the speaker button, ready to shut off the intercom the instant Khan said the wrong thing. "Now's your moment, Khan. Just speak from your cell. Uhura will ensure that your people receive you loud and clear."

Khan stiffened his shoulders. His deep voice passed through the force field, confident and commanding. Kirk held his breath.

"This is Khan, addressing the valiant crew of the *Botany Bay*. My brothers and sisters, your courage and ingenuity honors me. But we must choose our battles wisely, and now is not the time for warfare, not when we are so close to finally claiming what we set out to find so very long ago: a new world and a new beginning ...."

McGivers beamed at him. Kirk exhaled at last.

* * *

"Approaching Ceti Alpha V," Sulu reported from the helm.

"About time." McCoy leaned on the rail surrounding the command circle. The bruises on his neck were already fading. "Personally, I'm more than ready to see the backs of our guests."

"You and me both, Bones." Kirk contemplated the untamed class-M planet growing ever larger on the viewscreen. "What do you suppose Khan and McGivers will find there?"

Spock looked up from his science station. "Their destiny, I assume."

"Indeed," Kirk said. "Whatever that might be."

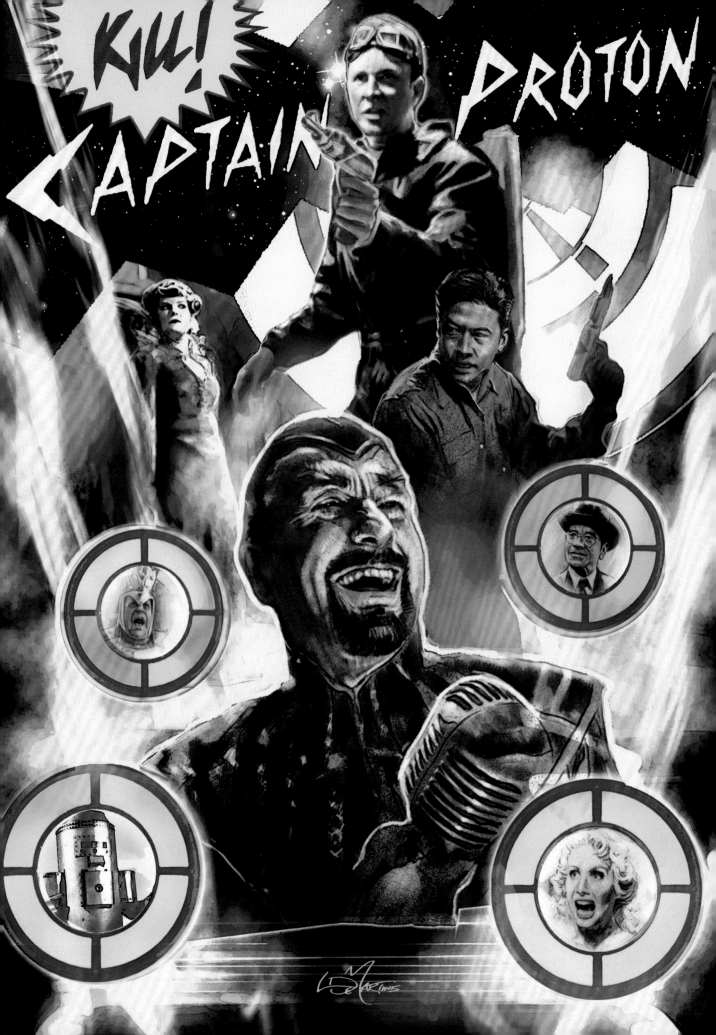

A *STAR TREK: VOYAGER* STORY

Kill Captain Proton!

STORY: LISA KLINK
ART: LOUIE DE MARTINIS

"I thought that giant crocodile thing was going to swallow us whole!" said ace reporter Buster Kincaid.

Captain Proton nodded as he adjusted the ship's course slightly. "It would have, if not for my trusty rocket pack."

The two friends smiled. Constance Goodheart, Captain Proton's loyal secretary, looked a little ill. She still had some of the monster's slobber in her golden hair.

They were in Captain Proton's rocket, flying past the rings of Saturn on their way back to Earth. He loved that view. It reminded him why he became a spaceman in the first place.

Suddenly a red light flashed on the control panel, signaling an incoming message. "Turn on the imagizer," he told Buster. "Let's see who's calling."

Buster activated the screen, revealing the face of Jonah Quimby, head of the Incorporated Planets Patrol. "Captain Proton, are you there?"

Proton leaned over to the imagizer. "Reading you loud and clear."

Quimby looked grim. "No time for pleasantries, Captain. I've just gotten word that Dr. Chaotica may be planning to steal some experimental technology from the Space Laboratory on Mars."

"Don't worry. We'll stop him."

"I know we can count on you," said Quimby, and signed off.

Captain Proton steered the ship toward Mars. "I hope you don't mind taking a little detour," he told the others.

"Of course not," Buster assured him.

As they approached the red planet, they could see the domed building that housed the Space Laboratory. Nearby was a landing pad, with one ship resting on it.

"That's Chaotica's ship," said Captain Proton. "He's definitely here."

He set down his rocket ship. He, Buster and Constance got out and approached the door to the laboratory. With his ray gun at the ready, Proton opened the door, unsure what he'd discover inside. He stepped inside, with his friends right behind him.

The first thing he saw was three scientists sitting on the floor, being guarded by Chaotica's chief henchman, Lonzak. The lab was dominated by a large bank of computing equipment, surrounded by work tables that held scientific equipment and mechanical parts. Chaotica was at one of these tables, holding up a long metal cylinder.

"Ah, yes, the amplitude modulator! The final piece of my greatest invention – the mind control ray!" He gave an evil laugh as he plugged the cylinder into the device on the table, which looked like a large ray gun.

Captain Proton strode forward. "The jig is up, Chaotica. Hand me that gizmo and let these people go."

"I don't think so," said Chaotica. He shouted an order: "Eliminate the intruders!"

His evil robot stepped out from behind the telescope and lumbered toward them, arms outstretched. It was a clunky, awkward thing, but virtually unstoppable. Constance screamed. Captain Proton and Kincaid both fired at the robot, but the energy bolts bounced off his metal skin harmlessly. The robot grabbed Constance by the arm and she screamed again. Proton rushed at the mechanical fiend and tried to pry its grip loose.

Chaotica used the moment

of distraction to pick up the mind control ray and shoot. The yellow beam hit Kincaid, making his entire body glow for a moment.

"Now you're under my control," Chaotica cackled. "I order you to kill Captain Proton!"

"Kill Captain Proton," Kincaid repeated dully, and fired his ray gun.

Constance let out a scream as Captain Proton dove to the side, avoiding the energy bolt. He came up behind one of the work tables as Kincaid fired again, vaporizing a rack of beakers. Proton had a clear shot at his friend, but couldn't bring himself to fire. "Buster, don't shoot! It's me!"

"I must obey," said Kincaid.

"No, you don't! You're not his slave. You're ace reporter Buster Kincaid!"

Chaotica watched with evil glee as Kincaid continued to advance toward Captain Proton, taking aim with his ray gun and firing. Captain Proton kept moving, ducking behind another table for cover.

"You don't want to do this, buddy," he said. "Think about all the years we've been friends."

Kincaid continued to advance, shooting energy bolts in his direction. Captain Proton took precise aim at his friend's ray gun and fired, knocking the weapon out of his hand. It clattered to the ground, fused into a lump of useless metal.

"No!" hissed Chaotica. "Kill him!"

"I must obey," said Kincaid. He picked up a heavy microscope from a work table and swung it at Captain Proton. Proton sidestepped, and reluctantly socked Kincaid in the gut, causing him to drop the microscope.

Captain Proton tried to get through to his friend. "I know you remember all the adventures we've had together. Like that time we escaped the sand sharks on the desert of Andromeda Prime."

FICTION

"I must obey." Kincaid lunged for the ray gun in Proton's hand. He grabbed his friend's wrist, and the two of them wrestled for control of the weapon.

Captain Proton kept talking. "What about when we rescued Constance from the ice dragon of Zatonia?"

He got the ray gun away from Kincaid, who then tackled him to the ground. They rolled around on the metal floor, each trying to gain the upper hand. Captain Proton was hampered by the fact that he didn't want to hurt his long time sidekick. "And when the Arkenians almost cooked us for dinner? You remember what you said?"

They crashed into a work table, spilling the contents. "You said, 'Sorry, Chief, we won't be serving you tonight.'"

Kincaid grabbed a loose piece of wire and wrapped it around Proton's throat. He struggled for breath, fighting to loosen the wire. "I couldn't have gotten through all of that without you. You're my... best... friend..."

"I must..." Kincaid began to say, then trailed off. His hands began to open, releasing the wire. He shook his head as if to clear it. Then he

THE CHIEF GUARD RUSHED AT PROTON, THE SHARP END OF HER PIKE AIMED AT HIS GUT.

looked Captain Proton in the eye. "You're my best friend, too."

Proton smiled, happy to have his friend back, and to be able to breathe again. They both turned to find that Chaotica had escaped during the fight, along with the robot and the mind ray. Even worse, he'd taken Constance.

Then one of the scientists stood up from where he'd been sitting with the others. "You have to stop him. He said that he's going use the amplitude modulator to create an even bigger mind control ray, one strong enough to enslave all of the people on Earth."

"He'll be going to the Fortress of Doom," said Captain Proton. "That's where he has his laboratory."

Buster nodded. "Planet X, here we come."

They returned to their rocket ship and flew toward Planet X, the dark, miserable ball of dirt that Chaotica called home. As they approached, Buster checked the scanner. "The lightning shield is up."

Captain Proton adjusted the ship's course. "Then I guess we won't be going in the front door. We'll have to set down on the planet and get in through the underground passageways."

He landed the ship in a clearing in a forested area near the entrance to the underground passageways. They had used these tunnels to get into the Fortress before. But Chaotica had now taken precautions to keep them out, by placing two guards near the mouth of the passageway. They were Lizard People, wearing metal armor and carrying long pikes – no ray guns in sight. Captain Proton and Kincaid seemed to have the advantage.

They stepped out from the trees, ray guns pointed at the Lizard People. "Stand aside and nobody needs to get hurt," Proton told them.

The chief guard hissed a laugh.

Then she told her companion, "Seize the intruders." Both guards advanced toward them.

"Have it your way," said Captain Proton, and fired at the chief guard. But to his surprise, the lizard's armor simply deflected the energy blast. Kincaid shot at another guard, with the same result. Their guns were useless!

The chief guard rushed at Proton, the sharp end of her pike aimed at his gut. He swiftly stepped aside to evade it. The second guard tried to impale Buster, who dashed behind a big tree.

Captain Proton spotted a large branch on the forest floor. He grabbed it just in time to block the lizard's next strike. Then, to his surprise, she opened her mouth and spat some kind of liquid at him. He instinctively raised his arm to shield his face and the spray landed on the sleeve of his jacket. The leather hissed where the venom touched it, dissolving away.

"It's poison!" he shouted to Kincaid. "Don't let it touch you."

The chief guard hissed at them. "Surrender, and we'll take you in alive."

"No deal." Proton swung the branch toward her head, but she knocked it aside with the pike. She spat at him again and he recoiled, barely avoiding the venomous spray.

Kincaid was successfully keeping the thick trunk of the tree between himself and the other guard. He picked up his own branch from the forest floor. He stopped and let the lizard get closer. As soon as his pike was in sight, Kincaid brought the branch down hard, knocking it out of the guard's hands. But as he reached out to pick up the pike himself, the guard spat venom at him, missing his face but spraying the back of his hand. Kincaid pulled back with a cry as the poison burned his skin.

Captain Proton blocked another strike by the chief guard. He swiftly dropped to the ground and used the tree branch to hit the back of the lizard's knees, knocking her off balance. She staggered back and fell. Proton struck her in the head with the branch. Then the guard lay still.

He turned to see Kincaid using his own branch to hold off the second guard. He managed to shove his scaly opponent back, putting a few feet between them. Proton aimed his ray gun at a large limb of the tree right above the guard's head. He fired an energy bolt, and the heavy limb fell, striking the lizard. Kincaid rushed forward, hitting him with the branch and knocking him out cold.

"Thanks," said Kincaid.

"Let's get moving before they come to," Proton suggested.

He led the way to the underground passages that ran under the Fortress of Doom. They moved carefully through the narrow, rocky tunnels, keep an eye out for more guards. They saw none.

Then they reached a large iron door. Working together, they managed to turn the wheel that opened the latch. Captain Proton pushed the heavy door open and they went inside the Fortress. They found themselves in Chaotica's infamous

CHAOTICA ONLY LAUGHED. "YOU'RE TOO LATE. THE MIND CONTROL RAY HAS ALREADY BEEN ACTIVATED."

Dungeon of Pain. Instruments of torture hung on the walls. Kincaid shuddered as they passed Chaotica's favorite device, the Cradle of Persuasion.

He and Proton walked through a narrow hallway and up a spiral staircase to the main level of the Fortress. Then they heard Constance Goodheart's distinctive scream.

Captain Proton ran toward the sound, with Kincaid right on his heels. They burst into Chaotica's laboratory, to find him standing beside a large device that looked like a space cannon, aimed out through the ceiling. Chaotica faced Constance, who was tied up nearby. "You'll learn to appreciate me, my dear, when you watch me turn the people of Earth into my faithful servants."

Then he spotted Captain Proton and Kincaid just inside the doorway,

ray guns in hand. "Proton!" he shouted in dismay. Then he turned to Kincaid. "I ordered you to kill him!"

"Your mind control is no match for the power of friendship," Kincaid told him.

Chaotica snarled. "Maybe with one man. But what are you going to do when I enslave your entire planet?"

"Can't let you do that," said Captain Proton.

Chaotica only laughed. "You're too late. The mind control ray has already been activated. It will fire in twenty seconds."

Sure enough, they could see large red numbers, counting down from twenty. Captain Proton approached the device while Kincaid held Chaotica at bay with his ray gun. Proton pulled open an access panel. Inside, he found a bewildering tangle of circuits and wires. "Remember what the scientist told us," said Kincaid. "He needed the amplitude modulator to make it work."

"So he did." Captain Proton pulled out wires, searching for the key piece of the machine as the counter continued to tick down. Fifteen seconds… fourteen… thirteen…

Then he saw the long metal cylinder Chaotica had stolen from the space laboratory. He reached in and tried to pull it out of the machinery, but it was solidly attached. Nine… eight… seven…

"Quick! Give me a hand!" he called.

Kincaid turned away from Chaotica and hurried over. He grabbed one end of the cylinder while Proton held the other. Together, they gave a mighty heave and the component finally popped free. The clock stopped with two seconds to spare.

They faced each other with a smile of relief. "Good to have you with me," said Captain Proton.

"Always," Kincaid replied.

Then they looked back to see that Chaotica had made his escape. This time, at least, he had left Constance behind. Captain Proton untied her and she gave him a kiss on the cheek.

The three of them returned to the rocket ship and blasted off, heading back to Earth for a well-deserved rest. At least, until Jonah Quimby of the Incorporated Planets Patrol called on them again… ✦

A *STAR TREK* STORY

Cumulative Damage

STORY: CHRIS DOWS

K irk strode down the Enterprise's empty corridors, thoughts and emotions battling for his attention. With the five-year mission over and his ship moored up in Starfleet's Earth-orbiting SpaceDock, uncertainty hung over Kirk like a damoclean sword. Most of the crew had disembarked days ago to enjoy their well-earned shore leave, relaxing while the Enterprise completed its routine refit. Others, such as McCoy and Spock, had left to contemplate their futures with Starfleet, leaving Kirk with the unthinkable prospect of his two closest friends not returning at all. If the uncertainty over his crew wasn't bad enough, no-one at Starfleet Command had even begun discussions with Kirk about his next assignment, and as he made his way towards the transporter room, for the briefest of seconds the lack of personnel and stillness of the ship reminded Kirk of the duplicate Enterprise to which the Gideons had spirited him away some months back. Shaking the feeling away, Kirk spotted the doors to Transporter Room Two, and focused his attention on the main issue at hand - the increasingly strange behaviour of Chief Engineer Montgomery Scott.

Kirk felt the hum of the transporter coils through the soles of his boots, signalling the system was active. As the doors swished open, he spied the redoubtable Scotsman, whose cryptic request to meet him in the transporter room had diverted Kirk from his tedious but vital shutdown protocols on the bridge. Kirk gave Scotty a puzzled smile, only to be met with an uncharacteristic frown and nervous tapping of fingers on the top of the transporter console. Kirk could immediately see something was wrong.

"Mister Scott. To what do I owe this mysterious invitation? Are we having a visit from the shipyard inspection team to discuss your final inspection report? Or are you having a crate of scotch beamed up and need a hand with it?"

Scotty looked down to the coordinate display, the soft cream light exaggerating the lines of worry in his expression.

"Not exactly sir, no. I… "

Scott kept his eyes lowered, his jaw set firm. Kirk's concern escalated.

"Scotty, what's wrong? You've not been on the bridge for more than a few minutes since we moored up, and I didn't see you for days on our journey home. Chekov was joking you'd spent more time in the Jeffries tubes than in your quarters, and Uhura told me you'd been carrying out almost continual surveys on every part of the ship – all on your own."

At the mention of Uhura, Scott looked uncomfortable. Clearly his attempts to hide his actions from his captain and friends had failed.

"Aye sir, that's true enough. I've had a lot to keep me busy."

Kirk frowned and stepped closer.

"Too busy to work with shipmates you've trusted for years or even take the time to talk with them?"

Kirk's tone was curt, forcing Scott to look up. His eyes were full of conflict and pain, something Kirk was all-too familiar with. Suddenly, he heard McCoy's voice in his head - 'this isn't the time to push, Jim.' Kirk softened his tone.

"We've all been out here a long time Scotty, got to know and understand each other like no other crew I've ever served with, and it's bound to have taken a toll. Believe me, if it was too painful to say goodbye to some of them, I understand."

Scott took a deep breath and sighed, the weight of the world – the universe, perhaps – on his shoulders.

"It's taken its toll alright, Captain. There's no denying that."

Before Kirk could ask what Scott meant, he was interrupted by a soft beeping from the console's communicator. Kirk nodded permission to Scott to activate it. An unfamiliar voice came through the speaker.

"Enterprise, this is Starfleet Command. One to beam up."

"Acknowledged. Energise."

Kirk stared at Scott for long seconds, only turning to the transporter dais behind him as the tone changed to signal final materialisation. A solitary humanoid figure quickly took shape, and as the system powered down Kirk was surprised to see Admiral Nogura standing before him, arms behind his back as was his manner.

"Ah, Jim. Welcome home."

Nogura stepped down onto the deck, hand extended in warm greeting. Kirk took it, feeling the power in the man's handshake despite his relatively small frame and advanced years. Kirk had known Nogura for most of his life, and while he was a friend to his family, he knew not to underestimate his keen intelligence and considerable experience – or to expect any favours despite their relationship.

"And Chief Engineer Scott. I'm assuming you've requested my presence to explain why your final report hasn't been submitted to the Corps? All highly irregular of course, but I'm willing to make allowances given your reputation."

Kirk turned to Scott, hiding his astonishment from Nogura. Given the time Scott had spent hidden away in every crevice of the Enterprise, for him not to have completed the report was unbelievable – and unforgiveable. Scott's gaze flicked from Kirk's glower over to Nogura's inquisitive frown.

"It's both of those things I need to talk with you about, Admiral – and yourself, Captain. I didn't want to submit my report without the opportunity to explain it – to explain myself - to the both of you."

Kirk could feel his sympathy for Scott evaporating. If there was one thing he hated, it was surprises – and right at that point in time, he didn't have a clue what was going on. But how did he question his Chief Engineer without looking a complete fool in front of Nogura? Why would Scotty *put* him in such a situation? Nogura strolled towards Scott and stood beside Kirk. Nogura's response mirrored Kirk's frustration.

"Engineer Scott, it looks to me as if you have a whole lot of explaining to do. I've heard of your protective nature towards the Enterprise and in truth, I've not met a Chief who wouldn't act the same. I know you've only been here a few days, but the clock is already ticking for the five-year overhaul and refit."

SCOTTY TOOK A DEEP BREATH AND SIGHED, THE
WEIGHT OF THE WORLD - THE UNIVERSE - PERHAPS -
ON HIS SHOULDERS.

Nogura's previous good humour had been replaced with flint, his words making Scott squirm like a fish on a hook. Kirk turned to Nogura in an attempt to take the focus off his engineer.

"How long are we looking at for the work, Admiral?"

Nogura looked around the transporter room.

"Oh, it shouldn't take longer than a few months, just a bridge module swap-out and a nacelle upgrade. Once we get the report."

Kirk saw the color drain out of Scott's face at the pointed reminder, and pressed on with his distraction.

"Good to hear. After my debrief and a few weeks' climbing, I'll be more than ready to get 'out there' again."

Nogura paused, seemingly looking for the right words.

"We'll talk about that another time."

Nogura's tone was evasive. Why did Kirk get the feeling there were now two people in the room not giving him the full picture? Scott cleared his throat, breaking the tension between the two.

"With all due respect Admiral, the repairs to the Enterprise are going to take a lot longer than a few months."

Kirk and Nogura spoke in unison. "*Repairs?*"

Scott sighed again. Kirk had never seen him look so… defeated.

"Aye, sirs. You'd best follow me. There's something you need to see."

The short journey to main engineering was taken in awkward silence, Scotty wisely choosing to remain tight-lipped and Nogura clearly not minded to expand on his previous remark. As the turbolift rapidly descended, Kirk could feel Nogura's impatience with the

situation growing. So, too, were his own anxieties over the Admiral's comment about his return to service and what mysterious revelations Scott was about to present. As the doors opened, Kirk fell in behind Nogura who followed Scott down the short corridor to the lower engineering level. By the time Kirk had entered the computer room annex, the engineer had already activated the angular viewscreen adjacent to the primary board and command desk.

"Take a look, Admiral. It doesn't make for pretty viewing."

Kirk looked over Nogura's shoulder to see an alarming – and unusual - pattern of lines overlaid on a deck plan of the Enterprise, all seemingly emanating from a point just behind where they stood. Scott's tone was hushed, as if he was a doctor breaking bad news to a patient.

"The schematic shows a network of micro-fractures in the outer

IT WAS TIME FOR KIRK TO DEFEND HIS ENGINEER AND HIS SHIP.

hull plating and inner supporting bulkheads. It extends to every point on the ship."

Kirk leaned forwards, scarcely able to believe his eyes.

"How… did this happen to my ship, Mister Scott?"

Scotty straightened up and pointed to the squat, grey cylindrical chambers on the floor of main engineering where the dilithium crystals were housed.

"It was that bloody Romulan cloaking device I fitted a way back Captain. I had a devil of a time with it, and had my doubts about potential effects on the ship at the time. Shortly after I removed it, I noticed fluctuations in the structural integrity field across the ship. At first, I put it down to the age of the old girl, but after our encounter with the Defiant and the Tholians, things just got progressively worse."

Nogura looked up from his scrutiny of the damage on the monitor.

"Was it the spatial interphase that did it?"

Scotty nodded slowly. Kirk wasn't surprised Nogura had read the mission report – he was renowned for being well-informed.

"Aye, sir. That's my best guess. That and emissions from the Tholian's web."

Kirk thought back to the report McCoy had given him on his return from drifting between realities, resisting a shudder at the recollection of his ghostly experience in his survival suit.

"The Doctor discovered the interphase distorted the molecular structure of brain tissue of those who were affected by that area of space. It's what sent the Defiant's crew and Chekov mad. Are you telling me it's the same for the Enterprise's hull?"

Scotty reached to the computer's controls and pushed another series of buttons. Interconnected blue-coloured blocks formed around the crazed lines, corresponding with their paths exactly.

"That's how it looks Captain. The only saving grace is it's restricted to components made of composite duranium."

Kirk snorted a laugh despite himself.

"Only? Come on Scotty, that's pretty much the whole exterior shell of the ship!"

The engineer looked to Kirk and shook his head sadly.

"Aye, sir. She's in a proper mess and no mistaking."

The room fell silent save for the humming of the impulse reactors powering the stationary vessel. Kirk watched Nogura as he clasped his hands behind his back and strolled out to the main engineering room, deep in thought. With Nogura out of earshot, Kirk turned to Scotty and grasped his arm.

"Scotty, why didn't you tell me what was going on?"

The engineer threw a glance over to Nogura then leaned forwards, whispering conspiratorially.

"Captain, if I'd detailed this in any report, you'd have been duty-bound to pass it on and they'd have towed us into SpaceDock like an old broken-down scow. I couldn't have that happen to her. I tried everything I could to seal the fissures, but nothing I did worked. I figured the fewer people knew about it, the better. I'm sorry to have put you on the spot, sir."

Kirk was about to give Scotty a lecture on how disappointed he was the engineer didn't feel he could trust his captain but thought better of it. Scotty was right. Despite how things had played out, it was time for Kirk to defend his engineer and his ship. The two left the computing station and walked over to Nogura, who was running his hand through his thick white hair as he stared at the spot where the Romulan cloaking device had been fitted to the deflector shield controls.

"Admiral, what are your thoughts?"

Nogura looked up to Kirk then over to Scott.

"It's not looking good for the Enterprise. While I cannot condone your subterfuge or theatrical approach Mister Scott, I can see why you wouldn't broadcast this information prior to arrival. The Corps of Engineers would have been sitting ready with cutting gear and blowtorches."

Kirk saw pain in Scott's face.

"Aye, Admiral. And that's why I wanted to talk with you here. She's a fine ship sir, and my other scans show her basic infrastructure is unaffected. I've already started work on the reconfiguration. She can be rebuilt from her bones, incorporating all the latest Starfleet systems, bigger and better than any ship in the fleet. She's worth the work, sir."

Scott's last sentence was said with absolute conviction. Nogura considered Scott's words then looked around the cavernous engineering space and nodded slowly.

"She is that, Mister Scott, but we'd be looking at a minimum of a couple of years... and a new captain."

Kirk felt his stomach lurch. Clearly Nogura had decided 'another time' to discuss his fate had arrived.

"What do you mean? If the Enterprise is going to be rebuilt, I need –"

Nogura's face hardened and eyes darkened. The change in his expression was enough for Kirk to stop talking.

"It's not what *you* need, Captain Kirk. It's what *Starfleet* needs. Good crews. Good ships. Experienced people who can train the next generation for whatever's out there. The refit that's being recommended would make this a virtually new vessel, and it'll take some convincing for me to get this approved – regardless of the extraordinary reputation you've all earned. If I can force the issue with Mister Scott's data, the Enterprise will be back – but not with you in charge."

Out of the corner of Kirk's eye, he could see the look of astonishment on Scott's face.

"Admiral Nogura, losing my ship is one thing, but losing my captain as well – "

"Mister Scott, you'll not be losing anything – particularly if your new Chief of Starfleet Operations adds his influential support to the refit."

Nogura looked pointedly at Kirk. There it was. Kirk's future all mapped out, tied in with the only way his ship was going to be saved. Nogura really was a formidable operator.

"Admiral... I don't know what to say. You know I want another starship command but..."

Nogura's eyes narrowed again. Kirk pressed on.

"...I'll take the post if it'll save my ship. I'd rather the Enterprise existed without me than not exist at all. I'll back the plan, but I want to choose a replacement captain who'll oversee the entire refit and work directly with Scotty. I'll stay a healthy distance away, but I'll want to be kept informed at every major stage. Agreed?"

The Admiral looked to Kirk, then to Scott, and around Engineering once again.

"I'm not in the habit of making deals Jim, but..."

Nogura turned, smiled, and offered his hand to Kirk.

"... this sounds like a good one."

Kirk shook it gratefully. Scotty smiled.

"Aye. A good one it is." ⭐

A STAR TREK STORY

Explorers of the Storm

STORY: PETER HOLMSTROM

"*Space is a dangerous place.*" As he had done countless times on his journey to Delta IV, Lieutenant Will Decker ran his father's final words through his head. Assigned as an attaché for an under-construction embassy without an ambassador, Decker expected he'd have many such opportunities.

Decker had spent his childhood dreaming of the day where he would join his father, the illustrious Commodore Matthew Decker, on grand adventures to the great unknown. That is, before his father died. *An intergalactic anomaly of immense destructive power*, the report said. An affidavit by Captain James T. Kirk of the Enterprise, citing Commodore Decker as a hero, but rumors of cowardice and even a mental breakdown were never far away.

"Approaching Delta IV. Security team on alert."

Lieutenant Decker straightened, ran a hand through his brownish-blonde hair, and turned to the Efosian Junior Lieutenant at the tactical station. A humanoid race, known for naturally hunched backs, long whiskers, and husky voices, one would believe them better suited to dark corners of an Orion slave market, rather than Starfleet. Though Starfleet constantly affirmed, appearances are never as they seem…

Delta IV's membership in the United Federation of Planets had only been ratified six months before, to the great consternation of a small demographic of the planet's population. Years of political debate and provincial membership did little to quell their displeasure at a Starfleet presence on the planet. Concern for stationed Starfleet officers on the planet was such, that a limited Embassy footprint was deemed appropriate. Decker was one of only a handful assigned to Delta IV, and ensuring the peace was essential.

"We've received a formal protest from the Embassy Liaison Officer. Seems they feel trust is greater than prudency..." Decker's back stiffened. He would have to discuss proper protocol with the liaison officer when he arrived... He tapped a communicator console near his station.

"Ensign Xon, report to the bridge." No response. Odd. "Ensign Xon?..."

With a transport this size, it didn't take Decker long to reach Ensign Xon's quarters. He reached up to--

"HAHAHAHAHAHAHAHA!!!" Decker's eyes widened. While few Vulcans were in Starfleet, one truth every cadet knew was, Vulcans do not laugh...

"Ensign Xon?!" The door opened and Ensign Xon stood before him, shaggy hair and youthful appearance could not hide the pointed ears and angular eyebrows. He was a Vulcan, but he was sweating profusely.

"Are you all right?" Decker asked earnestly.

"Yes, Lieutenant. I was... attempting to laugh." Decker didn't even try to hide his perplexity.

"... Laugh?"

"Yes, sir. The Vulcan control of their emotions has evolutionally altered their physiology. However, I elected to make the study of emotional connections of lesser species my focus at the Vulcan Science Academy."

"Are we... a petri dish to you, Ensign?"

"That would be inaccurate, sir. To understand the effects of the many, I seek a greater understanding of the all." If it wasn't for the Vulcan dispassion, Xon's answer would almost sound profound...

As the ship descended, Decker stared at the bright blue planet below. It might not be traversing the cosmos, charting unknown wonders, but this mission to Delta IV held a sense of adventure nonetheless. A new world, a mission to create a lasting and prosperous relationship between the Federation and the Delta people, and a place in the galaxy to call home...

Decker, Xon, and Bor-Deau marched down the clean sleek hallway of the Federation Embassy. Any awe and wonder Decker had at the beauty of Delta IV were quickly subverted by the realization the Federation

Embassy was sequestered miles away from anything... Federation or Deltan demand, Decker did not know, but was determined to bring it up to the liaison officer... among other things.

"Deltan physiology is quite distinctive to other races in the Federation," Ensign Xon observed. The red cushioned furniture and ornate colorful plants dotting the landscape reminded Decker of other Federation Outposts, despite the limited Starfleet and Deltan personnel on staff.

"I read the report on their psychic ability."

"*Psychic* is not accurate. Their emotions are represented physically through highly active pheromones, thus allowing others to experience the emotions as well."

"I was surprised to find a Vulcan requested this assignment, given..."

"Quite the contrary. This shall prove a fascinating exploration of the emotional experience. Into the deep pit, as humans say."

"Deep end, Mr. Xon," Decker said with a smirk.

Decker and Xon halted before the Operation Center of the Embassy. Straightening his gold uniform, Decker made his way inside.

Instantly, he was struck by a wave of irritation and aggression. Decker could feel his blood pressure rise and muscles tighten, as adrenaline rushed through his body.

"Phasers!" Images of attacking Deltan terrorists filled his mind. Even the Vulcan Ensign Xon was affected by whatever this was.

Decker's eyes shot around the room, but found only one occupant – a Deltan woman. Decker blinked, startled by her beauty. Through smoldering eyes, it struck Decker how the smooth, hairless head highlighted the depth of the eyes, and smoothness of the skin... She was beautiful, and she was angry.

DECKER EXTENDED HIS HAND, AND DID HIS BEST TO LOOK DISARMING.

"Lieutenant Decker, I presume? Since your scanning crews are gone, I take it they found no dangers?" Decker fought the urge to give in to the rage pounding through his body, but then noticed a gold Starfleet uniform...

"Unless you're injured, Ensign, superior officers are addressed as 'sir' when reporting for duty." The Deltan considered, then straightened in a salute posture.

"Ensign Ilia, Starfleet liaison officer assigned to Delta IV, reporting for duty, sir."

"Reported. Now, can you please tell us why my Vulcan friend is about to vomit?" Ilia's eyes widened as she registered Xon, hunched over in pain. As if a stream of water had just been cut off, Decker could feel his emotion start to recede.

"Apologies. I—"

"Mr. Xon?" Decker grabbed Xon's arm for support, unsure if a doctor was on staff.

"Forgive me, sir. I seem to have an adverse reaction to Deltan pheromones. I must go to my quarters." Without waiting for approval, Xon exited.

"It seems I've made a bad impression."

"More than one, Ensign." Decker could feel his anger rising, but couldn't be sure if it was from his own doing or not.

"What has happened is Starfleet is treating my planet as a threat, rather than an ally."

"You are part of that Starfleet unless I'm mistaken." Ilia allowed herself a moment to glare before softening.

"Yes, sir. I meant not to offend you personally, but to question the rationale of the action." Decker considered the Deltan before him. An image of his father, austere in body and soul, standing on a porch of their family home, about to tell his son yet again of another long assignment away from home, entered Decker's mind. He let out a sigh and forced a slight smile.

"Forgive me, Ensign. I believe we got off on the wrong foot. I apologize for any feeling of intrusion our security team conveyed. With the recent threats on the part of the Deltan people against Starfleet, thorough security was necessary. My name is Lieutenant Will Decker." He extended his hand, and did his best to look disarming. Ilia responded with a cool stare.

"Sometimes you have to take a leap of faith first. The trust part comes later..."

Decker spent the next few weeks trying to soften the situation with his new liaison officer, to little effect. Though in rare instances he would find her staring at him. Whether out of curiosity or animosity, was anyone's guess. It was only after his office was settled and a semblance of routine was established, did he feel comfortable addressing some lingering questions.

"Your body chemistry is not conformed to Deltan physiology, it reacted poorly to my emotional state. Deltan pheromones are a tangible representation of emotional states. Thus, when we are joined as lovers, family, or friends, we are connected on a profound level."

"Starfleet reports were scant, but seemed to indicate we'd have nothing to worry about."

"Deltans have trained for years to prepare for interspecies communication, but it is still a new concept. I regret to say I forgot my training."

"And yet you joined Starfleet?"

"As a child, I dreamed of space travel. Read books of your world... Horatio Hornblower? Adventures of the high seas. I must admit, you look much as I imagined him." She smiled. "While some of my people believe joining the Federation was a mistake, most see it as a dawning of a new age."

Perhaps I'm finally getting through to her.

"The First Age the Deltan people explored the stars. The Second Age we turned inward and improved our minds. Closed off from the rest of the galaxy, our people stagnated. With the joining of the Federation, we entered the Third Age."

"Perhaps..." Ilia's head darted away. "What is it?"

Fear covered the Deltan's face.

"The grounds... terror."

Ilia rushed ahead as Decker's own fear grew.

Outside the Embassy, pandemonium ensued...

Wave after wave of burn marks *seared* the ground from an unseen power. As if an invisible pendulum swung destruction from on high. Deltans and Starfleet officers ran for cover, or searched for answers.

"A new age, Ensign..?" Decker rushed back to the Ops Center to notify Starfleet command of a terrorist incursion. Ilia rushed behind.

"You don't know this was my people!"

"Those screams say otherwise! You're relieved, Ensign."

"At a time of crisis, you need all Starfleet officers available." Entering Ops, she took her station at environmental controls. Other stations remained empty with the exception of Lieutenant Bor-Deau at security, either an officer yet to report, or caught outside in the maelstrom of energy. Decker thought of contesting Ilia, but then thought it better to keep an eye on her.

"Scan for other disturbances on the planet."

"None. It seems to be localized to this facility," Ilia offered, knowing it didn't bode well for her case. *Of course. How could it be anything other than an act of terrorism,* Decker thought.

"Are Embassy shields operational?" Decker barked at Bor-Deau.

"Shields have been neutralized."

"Neutralized? How?"

"Unknown, Sir."

Decker stared at his sensor readout. The display glitched and sputtered out.

"My readout is malfunctioning."

"Mine is still operational, sir." Ilia piped in. *Damn.* Until better information arrives, he'd have to trust her.

"Status."

"No sonic interference, energy distortions, or gravitational fluctuation." *This doesn't make sense...*

Decker tried to think of what his father would do in this situation...

"I have to see what's going on. Notify Starfleet Command."

"And the local officials!" Ilia offered.

"Inform them *both*, we're under attack." Bor-Deau nodded.

Decker dashed outside to find mayhem remained. Scorch marks tore through the grounds, as waves of "something" undulated through the air.

"It must be some kind of creature!" As Decker reached for his phaser, he noticed something. The undulating waves were crashing against the shields...

"The shields are up..." Ilia saw it too.

"Malfunction?" As Ilia said it, Decker saw something materialize beside him. Something that shouldn't be. Something that couldn't be.

"Dad?"

Ilia turned to Decker.

"Lieutenant?" Decker didn't answer, transfixed by the image of his father. "What do you see?" Commodore Matthew Decker: husky, stern jaw, with sad eyes that have seen too many winters. He seemed to be crying, in pain. *DON'T YOU THINK I KNOW THAT?* Decker heard his father say. At least, he thought he did... Neither sound nor vibration came through the air.

"It's my father... He's in pain, dying."

"There's nothing there, Lieutenant."

"No, he's..." Decker reached out to his father, but his hand passed right through.

"Why would you see your father?" Decker stared at the waves, cutting larger and larger ribbons into the grounds.

"Bor-Deau with the shields, my readouts malfunctioning, and now my father. It's playing into our greatest fears!" He sees the ribbons again, each one growing outward, as if emanating from a central source.

"Quick, back inside!"

Decker and Ilia rushed back to Ops

A SMALL SMILE CAME OVER DECKER'S FACE, AND HE WAS PLEASED TO SEE IIIA SMILE IN RETURN.

"Bor-Deau, scan the grounds and correlate the scorch marks in the earth. See if there's a pattern." Bor-Deau punched up a schematic of the Embassy. The lines of scorched grounds created consecutive circles. "Extrapolate the existing rings, factoring in distance and growth. Are they emanating from a central location?" The computer worked quickly, indicating a small dot within the Embassy itself: the living quarters.

"If that's the center, the hallucinations may be more intense the closer we get." Ilia locked eyes with Decker. "Are you sure you can handle it?"

"Suppose we'll have to take a leap of faith?" A small smile came over Decker's face, and he was pleased to see Ilia smile in return.

Rushing through the halls of the Embassy, Decker, Ilia, and Bor-Deau drew weapons. Decker could feel the emanations now physically. Pain, suffering, beyond what he thought possible. He and Ilia slam into the wall.

"Bor-Deau, get out of here!" Another wave hits them, this time bringing images of his father, the destruction of a shuttlecraft, and a

meaningless death into his mind. Ilia reached out her hand and touched his shoulder, releasing calming pheromones into his body, forcing him to relax.

"Will… Whatever is causing this pain, you have to let it go." Decker's breath comes in short and staccato even with the pheromone rush. The walls around him close as wave after wave crash through.

"My father. Died, in space. Away from everything, all alone... A meaningless death."

"You're not alone now…" Decker saw the truth in Ilia's words. A glimmer of hope in the otherwise empty hall.

Together, Decker and Ilia inched forward, until they reached the center. Decker smashed the door pad, and crawled through the opening to find –

Ensign Xon! Silently and peacefully sitting in the center of the room, with his hand on an equally silent and peaceful-looking Deltan.

"XON!!!" Xon blinked to awareness and stared lazily at Decker. The Deltan offered a similar gaze, neither remotely aware of anything amiss. The waves

instantly stopped, and the soothing hum of Embassy air returns.

"Is everything all right, sir?"

"I don't believe embarrassment is in the Vulcan vocabulary, but…" Decker smiled, while meeting with Ilia the next day.

"He wouldn't have known a mind-meld with a Deltan would cause such a catastrophe of psychic energy. One presumes oil and water do not mix."

"He should have used his head. I shall have to report this…"

"Perhaps you should use your heart, Lieutenant. No one was hurt. He will learn, as we all will.

"Perhaps in working together to overcome this crisis, we've set a path for our two cultures to co-exist?"

"Perhaps we have." Ilia smiled. "Here, I have something for you." She handed him a photograph a 19th-century sailing ship in a storm. "A welcoming gift."

"Explorers of the Storm." Decker smiled in return, content in the moment it gave. Nevertheless, Decker turned to stare out the window, to the blue sky on the horizon, and the stars that lay beyond… ⌄

Prey

STORY: LISA KLINK

ILLUSTRATION: LOUIE DE MARTINIS

"I have tried restricting his privileges and sending him to his room," said Worf. "And yet I still catch him stealing."

Dr. Beverly Crusher was sympathetic. "I know it's been difficult. But Alexander needs time to adjust to life on the *Enterprise*."

"What did you do to punish Wesley when he was this age?"

"After he lost his father, Wesley decided it was time for him to become an adult." She smiled ruefully at the memory. "He didn't have much of a rebellious stage."

The Klingon grunted in response. He checked the readout on the shuttle's navigation system. "We are approaching Amara."

Amara was the thirty fourth moon of Delos. While Captain Picard and several senior officers attended a diplomatic conference on the planet's surface, Beverly was on her way to collect samples of a native plant with medicinal properties, which only grew on Amara. The Delosians had warned her that the moon was home to hostile creatures known as qanaths, so Worf had offered to come along to protect her. She suspected that he had volunteered for this mission at least partly to get out of the conference on Delos.

"There are storms in the upper atmosphere. Prepare for turbulence as we land," Worf cautioned her.

She looked at the small moon through the view screen. It was covered by clouds, which crackled with bolts of lightning. The electromagnetic storms had prevented them from transporting to the surface. It also made for a bumpy ride as Worf took them down into the clouds. Hit by lightning on all sides, the shuttle jostled fiercely. Too fiercely, thought Beverly, as she struggled to stay in her seat.

Her companion seemed to agree. "The storms are too violent. I'm taking us back into orbit."

But before they could escape the atmosphere, the shuttle was struck by the most powerful bolt of lightning yet. It rocked sharply and went suddenly silent.

Worf checked a panel. "The engines are dead." He pressed several buttons on the control panel.

"Propulsion systems are off line," the computer announced. Worf muttered a Klingon curse. He turned to the doctor. "Brace for impact."

The shuttle broke through the cloud layer and glided toward the surface of the moon. It skimmed across the thick foliage that covered the ground, slowing down as it broke through treetops, snapping heavy branches as it went. Beverly was thrown forward. She raised her arm to protect her face as she smacked hard against the console. She felt a bone in her right forearm break. Worf was jolted out of his seat, hitting his head against the wall. He collapsed.

The shuttle continued to descend through the jungle. It struck the muddy ground, sliding forward until it came to rest in a clearing. In the abrupt quiet, Beverly lay still for a moment, counting herself lucky to be alive. Then she looked over at Worf. She didn't see him breathing and thought for a sickening moment that he'd been killed. Then he groaned and tried to sit up.

She saw a large wound on his head, bleeding profusely. "Don't move. You're hurt," she told him.

"Are you all right?" he asked.

"Mostly." As she picked her way across the cabin to retrieve the emergency medical kit, she could feel bruises all over her body, but only her arm seemed to be broken. She got the kit and returned to Worf. Of course, he was now sitting up. Klingons really were the worst patients.

"Stay still," she told him, as she took out the medical tricorder with her left hand. She scanned him. He had broken several small bones in his wrist, but that wasn't the worst of it. "I'm detecting some bleeding in the brain."

She rooted around in the emergency kit and came up with the dermal regenerator, then ran it over his head wound, sealing it up. Next she found the osteo-regenerator and used it to heal his wrist. Beverly also ran it over her own broken arm, feeling the bones knit together. She'd do a full scan on herself later, when they were safely back on the ship.

"Unfortunately, this equipment isn't sophisticated enough to use for brain surgery," said Beverly. "I have to get you back to the Enterprise medical bay." And quickly, she thought, before that brain bleed causes irreparable damage.

She looked out the front view screen and saw the front of the shuttle hopelessly damaged by the crash. They weren't lifting off anytime soon. She turned to the comm system and pressed a button to transmit. "This is shuttle *Cochrane* calling the *Enterprise*."

"Communications are off line," the computer told her in that maddeningly calm voice.

"Analysis," she requested.

"The isolinear circuits of the long range transmitter have been damaged."

"We can use circuitry from other systems to replace them," said Worf. He started to stand. "I will do the repairs."

She shoved the big Klingon back down. "You'll do no such thing. The more you move,

the greater the chances of permanent brain damage. I'll take care of it."

He looked at her. "The long range transmitter can only be accessed from the exterior of the shuttle."

She knew that the atmosphere on this moon was unbreathable. She also remembered what the Delosians had told them about the qanaths. Carnivorous, flying beasts large enough to carry off human prey. But the repairs still needed to be done.

"I'll bring a phaser," she told him.

Worf got unsteadily to his feet. "I won't let you take that risk."

"And I won't let you risk your health." She tried to get in his way as he walked toward the

back of the shuttle, but he just moved her aside. He opened a compartment and removed an extra-vehicular activity suit.

"I will be fine," he insisted.

"No, you won't." But he was already starting to put on the suit. Beverly needed to take more drastic action. She went to the emergency medical kit and pulled out a hypospray of sedative. "I'm sorry about this," she told him, as she administered the spray to his neck.

Worf looked at her in angry surprise as his legs gave out and he sank to the floor. She scanned him and found his life signs stable. But that brain bleed was still progressing. She didn't have a lot of time to get them rescued.

She opened another compartment and took out a

BEVERLEY WHIRLED AROUND TO FACE A VULTURE-LIKE THING WITH A THREE METER WINGSPAN...

tool kit. Inside, she found the screwdriver she needed to remove the access panel under the shuttle's main console. She unscrewed the panel, revealing the isolinear circuitry beneath. "How many circuits in the long range transmitter are damaged?" she asked the computer.

"Three," the mechanized voice answered.

Beverly removed four circuit chips, just to be sure. She placed them in the tool kit. She retrieved the second EVA suit and climbed into it, adjusting the fit as she went. Even so, the suit was bulky and uncomfortable. And despite oxygen flowing in from the life support pack, she found it somehow harder to breathe.

Beverly stepped into the shuttle's airlock and closed the door to the main cabin. Then she opened the exterior hatch.

Tool kit in one hand and phaser in the other, she ventured out onto the surface of the moon. It was muddy, sucking at her boots as she took each step. She looked around the open clearing and up at the dull pink sky. No hostile flying creatures in sight.

"Where is the access panel for the long range transmitter?" she asked the computer.

"The rear access panel is located half a meter forward of the left engine."

Beverly went to the designated spot on the shuttle's hull and found the panel. Despite the awkward gloves on her hands, she managed to open it. Inside, she could see the damaged circuitry. Because of the EVA suit's helmet, she didn't hear the sound of wings flapping until it the creature was almost on top of her.

She whirled around to face a vulture-like thing with a three meter wingspan and a body the size of a horse. The long, sharp beak snapped at her.

The doctor screamed and instinctively ducked. She dropped the toolkit and brought up the phaser, firing at the qanath. It let out an ear-piercing cry as the beam hit its feathered bulk. But it didn't stop coming, raising a razor-tipped talon and sinking its claws into her shoulder. Beverly felt the creature starting to lift her off the ground. She fired again, this time at the qanath's eye. It released her with a screech and backed off. Air began to rush out of the holes in

her EVA suit. Another qanath dove out of the sky. She shot at it and made a run for the hatch, barely slipping into the airlock before the snapping talons could grab her.

Shaking and breathless, she vented the toxic air from the airlock before opening the door to the main cabin. She pulled off the helmet and inhaled deeply. Then she heard one of the qanaths land on the roof of the shuttle, claws clicking against the metal hull. She thought about the damage to the ship and wondered if it would be able to find an opening. She had to get herself and Worf out of here. And quickly.

It would take too long for the Enterprise crew to notice they were gone and start looking for them, so waiting around for rescue wasn't an option. She briefly considered waking the Klingon. He could shoot the qanaths while she installed the new isolinear circuitry. But the exertion would only cause more internal bleeding. She scanned him with the medical tricorder and found that the blood leaking inside his skull was already causing pressure on his brain. She had to let him rest. Beverly needed to get back out there and finish the repair herself. But how?

She slipped out of the top half of the suit, checking the damage from the creature's claws. She found four holes in the arm, along with matching punctures in her shoulder. Repairing herself with the dermal regenerator

was quick work. Now she had to fix the suit. She searched the various compartments in the shuttle until she found a tube of sealant, presumably meant to repair minor cracks in the hull. It would have to do. She used the sealant to close the holes in the EVA suit and gave it some time to dry.

She knew there was one qanath on the roof, and at least one more of them out there. Probably more. She had her phaser, but wasn't confident in her ability to fend off the creatures before they tore her apart. Could she use the shuttle's weaponry somehow? She didn't think the placement of the phasers would allow her to reach the one on the roof. And she wouldn't be able to fire them while she was out doing the repair. She also couldn't detonate a torpedo so close to the damaged shuttle without destroying it. Brute force might be Worf's answer to the dilemma, but Beverly had to find another way.

Could she chase them away somehow? She considered electrifying the hull, which would probably drive off the qanath sitting on top of the shuttle. But it wouldn't stop any others from swooping in and grabbing her. Maybe she could replicate some kind of toxin or sedative, spray it in the air around the shuttle to keep the beasts at bay. Unfortunately, she knew nothing about their anatomy, or what kind of chemicals might harm them.

She heard the thing on the roof moving around, pecking at the hull, presumably looking for weaknesses. The sound reminded her of hearing rats in the attic of her grandmother Felisa's house in the colony of Arvada III. Felisa had tried trapping the rats, then concocted her own poisons, but the rodents refused to be exterminated. She'd finally set up little devices which emitted an ultrasonic sound that the rats couldn't stand. They had left the attic to find a new home somewhere more hospitable. Could the same idea possibly work with the qanaths? She wouldn't have to keep them away permanently, only long enough for her to replace three isolinear chips.

Beverly knew that the highest sound humans could hear was approximately 20 kilohertz, which was fairly low among Earth's animals. She'd start with a higher frequency. "Computer, vibrate the ship's hull at a frequency of one hundred kilohertz."

She couldn't hear the vibration herself, of course, but what she was listening for was any reaction from the qanath on the roof. She only heard it continuing to walk back and forth, tapping the hull with its beak. "Raise it to five hundred kilohertz," she told the computer.

The creature let out a pained screech and Beverly heard its wings flap as it flew away. She smiled. Maybe this would actually work. She checked the holes in the EVA suit and found them sealed. She quickly donned the suit and went back out through the airlock.

She cautiously stuck her head outside, searching for any sign of the flying beasts. She saw several circling at some distance from the shuttle. The doctor quickly returned to the panel she'd removed from the hull. She pulled out the three damaged isolinear circuits, then picked up her abandoned tool kit and retrieved the intact circuits. She turned to look at the qanaths and thought that the big one had ventured a little closer. She knew that hunger would soon outweigh its discomfort with the ultrasonic sound. With her hands encased in the awkward gloves of the suit, she inserted each of the new circuits into the long range

transmitter. Sweat ran into her eyes and she couldn't wipe it away. She blinked, trying to see well enough to finish her task. The last circuit went in. She quickly closed the access panel and screwed it shut. Then she started for the hatch.

As if sensing that its meal was about to get away, the massive qanath dove at her. She fired the phaser at the creature's wing. The energy bolt hit, but the qanath kept coming. She shot it again and the creature fell to the ground. Beverly hurried into the airlock, drained the air, and stepped into the shuttle.

She gratefully removed the helmet and wiped her sweaty face. Then she went to the console and hit the comm link again. "*Enterprise*, this is Shuttle *Cochrane*. Do you read me?"

She'd never been so glad to hear a voice as she was to hear Data's now. "We read you."

"Worf is hurt and we need immediate evac," said Beverly. "Tell the medical team to prep for emergency surgery."

"Understood," he replied.

"I'm turning on the locator beacon. Be careful taking a shuttle to the surface," she cautioned. "The electromagnetic storms made us crash."

"I will pilot the rescue craft myself."

"And bring a security team. There are hostile creatures here," she told him.

"Affirmative. What is your condition, Doctor?"

She considered this. "I'm all right. Ready to get out of here."

With immense relief, she turned away from the console and went to check on Worf. He was already beginning to regain consciousness.

"The rescue team is on the way," Beverly told him. She scanned him with the tricorder. "The bleed is pretty bad, but I can take care of it once we get you back to the ship."

He grunted groggily in response. She knew that was as much thanks as she was going to get for saving them both. As for the medicinal plants she'd come here to collect, she'd just have to do without them. ✦

EXCLUSIVE FICTION

Growing Pains

WORDS: PETER HOLMSTROM
ART: LOUIE DE MARTINIS

P ain… The first glint of awareness was always the same. Childhood dreams of blissful joy faded, transitioning to a dull throbbing on each side of the temple.

For a moment, he let himself believe the dream was real – perhaps the childhood in Mogadishu, Somalia, was real, and he'd awaken to find his mother and father back from an exozoology mission. He would be well. But, as it had done many mornings before, the dream faded, the dull pain remained, and Lieutenant, Junior Grade, Geordi La Forge sat up in bed.

Geordi instinctively rubbed the side of his head, knowing it would only make the throbbing worse, but unable to stop himself. He had slept on his temple again, right where the VISOR connection to his skull would be made. An instinct to protect a wounded area? Or perhaps his body's desire to draw attention to the pain, and notify appropriate departments to help thwart infection. The unintended pain came with the VISOR, with no cure.

Doctor Crusher tried to tell him as much when he first reported to the *Enterprise*, three months before.

"I see two choices. The first is painkillers—"

"—Which would affect how this works. No. Choice number two?"

"Exploratory surgery. Desensitise the brain areas troubling you."

"Same difference. No, thank you, Doctor…"

It had been a long shot, of course. Even Doctor Beverly Crusher, one of the best and brightest of the Federation, wouldn't have a miracle cure which no other medical textbook had. Still, he'd allowed himself a glimmer of hope. Instead, he received another sympathetic shrug of the shoulders.

That conversation rolled through Geordi's head as he strolled through a lush forest on the planet Ruan IV, with an away team from the *Enterprise*.

"How much further, Minister?" Commander Riker asked the amphibian minister leading the charge. The Federation had been contacted by the Ruan IV with promises of powerful medical resources, if a trade treaty could be reached.

"Thessss temple isss ahead, Comandderrrr."

The planet had a long history of religious activity tied to nature. Yet, there was no denying, the claims of medical miracles from the natural plant life were… intriguing.

Despite extensive education in antimatter power and dilithium regulators at the Academy, Geordi accepted a helmsman position on the *Enterprise* – no better way to be on the front lines of the latest discoveries, both for technological advancements, and maybe… just maybe… a cure for himself…

Geordi's red and black uniform bounced off the multi-colored display of plant life around him. Unlike the natural sight experienced by other humans, Geordi's VISOR subverted his blindness to translate the visual landscape into complex electrical signals directly to the brain. He could see… everything. The whole range of the EM Spectrum, translated by his VISOR, to his brain. Color, sound, heat, and even vibrations coalesced into a wide symphony of inputs.

Security chief Tasha Yar strolled up.

"I always thought the Federation was a secular system, yet here we are negotiating with a people that prides themselves on their religious heritage. Why?" Geordi always found Tasha's voice the most soothing of the crew. While he didn't technically have the frame of reference to know what humans described as objectively beautiful from a visual perspective, he imagined her to be a very beautiful person.

Geordi shrugged. "Hope? Hope of something better, left undiscovered."

"Arrrivvveeeddd," The Minster indicated from the front of the party. Geordi stood before a large ornate temple, spread into the side of a mountain. The temple seemed to be made of plants, each flower, fungi, and bush ungulated in unison, as if connected.

"Theysssss heallsssss."

As they neared the Temple, Geordi was hit with a cacophony of visual input. "Commander, I…" Every wave, from sound to light to heat, crashed into Geordi's VISOR in ways he'd never seen before. "Whoa… Would you look at that."

"What is it, Geordi?" Data asked. Geordi focused on the android, finding comfort in the almost total lack of VISOR inputs from his lifeless friend.

"Everything is... changed. This temple has a very different resonance frequency than any I have ever seen."

"Recommend caution, sir. This may be a trap." Tasha's soundwaves cut through the cacophony like cool water, giving an anchor of normality to latch onto.

"Noosssss... issss sacred placccceeee," the minister reassured.

"Commander, if these lifeforms are truly different than anything we have seen, the possibilities for scientific advancements would be significant," Data countered.

The pain through Geordi's temple increased. Perhaps something associated with the planet? Perhaps just his imagination.

"Are they safe to harvest? Scientific study will be required before a trade deal can begin." Riker authoritatively proclaimed. The Minister nodded and bowed.

Geordi did his best not to show his discomfort. "Sir, I'd like to assist with the sample analysis. I think my VISOR readouts may be useful." Tasha's body temperature rose, clearly not pleased with this support of a potential threat.

"Do it." Riker nodded towards Tasha. "Hopefully this mission proves uneventful."

It was... on the planet.

Geordi and Tasha strolled down the corridor of the *Enterprise* some days later.

"Laboratory duty. Not a bad way to take a vacation," Tasha chaffed. Geordi let out a wide smile and laughed.

"Hardly. Excited to get my hands dirty. Remember, my training was in engineering, and my parents were scientists."

Geordi stopped before Cetacean Ops. Starfleet usually designed entire ships for aquatic lifeforms, but the appeal of serving on the *Enterprise* traversed more than just humanoids. Cetacean Ops was especially built for aquatic organisms, with water of various salinity to accommodate different lifeforms.

"Well, hope you have a good time with the fishes. I'll be practicing my Anbo." Geordi smiled, but pushed thoughts of Tasha in the holo-gym out of his mind as the door opened to –

An observation room pulsating with sound vibrations, shaking the glass with rhythmic regularity.

Lieutenant Soaf-ie, a Selkies of the planet, Pacifica, floated in the center of a large tank... asleep and doing the underwater equivalent of... snoring.

Geordi turned to Tasha with a look of puzzlement, only to see Tasha inch away in a stance of mock-nervous caution.

"Good luck." She whispered, and was gone. Geordi turned back to the tank, and strolled forward.

"Hello?" Nothing. Frustrated, he reached up, and knocked on the observatory window.

Soaf-ie shuddered awake, ripples of the scales giving a wispy appearance to the mermaid-like scientist.

"Pardon me, I was conducting an experiment." The high-frequency melodies used for communication turned to basic and they passed through the translator on the nearby wall.

"An experiment in wasting time?" Soaf-ie cocked her head to one side, and Geordi had the distinct impression she was staring directly into his soul.

"Sorry, I didn't mean – I'm just excited to get started."

Geordi turned to stare at a laboratory stasis pool, where a number of plant species from the planet now resided. Unlikely to last long in the *Enterprise* environment, submerging the samples in a stasis tank of water seemed appropriate.

"Speed and excitement are not the scientific way, Lieutenant," Soaf-ie said silently.

Days went by with little success. For reasons unknown, it took many configurations for the sensors to even register the plants' existence. Geordi's excitement grew at the thought of new discoveries.

"The molecular structure of these samples is extraordinary."

"What do you see, Lieutenant?" Soaf-ie floated in the observation tank above, connected to the lab stasis pool by a small inlet pipe.

"It's Geordi, please." He adjusted the display to show Soaf-ie. "Variations of wave patterns on every level."

"And these plants have medicinal properties?"

"That's the claim."

"A long journey is ahead of us. One of patience, and small rewards." Geordi's head throbbed. He'd had this pain all his life, but it seemed to be getting worse. Could there be a connection? Or just his own imagination…

"What if we kick it with antimatter radiation?" Soaf-ie merely floated in the water like a judgmental angel.

"We break the plants down into their molecular base, and build them back up from there."

"Antimatter radiation is dangerous. As an expert, you should know that."

"But as an expert, I know what it can handle. Think about it. Working from the outside in could take years—"

"Decades, if proper scientific procedure is followed."

"But why wait when we can unlock the secrets of these organisms right here?! Think of all the people we can help."

"You're pushing too hard, Lieutenant, and could contaminate the samples."

"I don't think so." Geordi marched to the control console and began punching in keys.

"We have yet to gain any readings, you don't know what radiation will do."

Geordi queued up a burst of antimatter radiation, and activated a containment field to keep the samples in check. "Science is about taking chances, and making mistakes."

Soaf-ie swam right to the protective glass and smashed her fist against it.

"No, Geordi, that—" Geordi wasn't listening. Excited, at last, to be doing something.

Geordi punch the key and activated the antimatter radiation, only to find…

Nothing. The plants were neither affected nor dismantled by the radiation. Not even a shudder.

Then, Geordi noticed something…

Subatomic. Division.

"Geordi? What is it?"

"That's not possible." Geordi looks to the console for confirmation, but sensors maintained nominal readings. Yet Geordi's VISOR told him differently.

> "SCIENCE IS ABOUT TAKING CHANCES AND MAKING MISTAKES."

"The structure of the plants are changing on a subatomic level. They're in a state of quasi-molecular flux?..."

"Dimensional alteration?"

"No. They're… growing."

Even now, Geordi could see small spindles of green sprout from the plant samples.

"Spontaneous cell division is highly unlikely."

"Tell that to them…" Geordi checked the containment field, still at full power, but the plants were growing rapidly.

"Decontaminate!"

"The containment field is holding. We can still get vital information."

"Its growth is unexplainable, do not let your own desire for answers blind you to the dangers of the situation."

Geordi ignored the warning. His VISOR was processing information at a rate he never thought possible. Images distorted, as the onslaught of the alien waves emanating from the plants became overpowering.

"Lieutenant!" Geordi snapped back to consciousness, not even realizing he'd disassociated, to find the containment field had been breached. Spindly tendrils of plant matter flowed through the field as if it wasn't even there, and were now venturing into the Cetacean Ops tank itself. Soaf-ie was at her control console, staring back as vines grew larger.

Geordi gritted his teeth.

"Computer, reinforce the containment field." The field hummed, but rather than cutting off the growth, the vines shuddered and grew thorns, each releasing a brownish liquid in their wake.

Geordi's mind raced for an answer, as toxins inched closer to Soaf-ie with each passing moment.

"Computer! Emergency contact the Minster of Ruan IV." The communication display lit up with the sleepy Minister.

"Sssss-whattttsss?"

"Minister, our plant samples are growing out of control, how can we stop it?!" The Minister stared perplexed.

"Whyss wouldss wess knows? To question, isss to doubts the godss. Thiss isss blasssphhemmyyy." Geordi cut the comm channel in frustration, and stared around.

"Lieutenant…" Geordi looked toward the observation tank as Soaf-ie lost consciousness. Its once clear liquid now strewn with massive viperous vines, expanding in every direction.

"No!"

"Geordi? What's going on?!" Tasha Yar barked out as she and a security team entered. Her face turned to terror before the mountain of swimming horror. "Oh no… Phasers ready. That water pressure is enough to destroy this section, no firing until I give the order!" Shame washed over Geordi at what he had done.

"I can fix this, hang on!" Geordi looked at the console, which only moments before read nominal readings as he programmed the computer to emit a low-level antimatter radiation burst. The console still read nominal…

"No sensor readings… affected by strong containment fields… The plants must feed off antimatter radiation! A low-level burst of ion radiation may counteract it."

Geordi moved to the tank and opened the entry hatch.

"Not the time for a dip, Geordi!" Tasha yelled.

"I have to get her out! Ion radiation could kill her."

"The exits are jammed!"

"I'll make one." Geordi grabbed a phaser from Tasha. "Trust me, please." Tasha nodded solemnly.

Geordi returned to the hatch, the thorned vines nearly as big as his arm swinging menacingly through the water. He clocked the rotation of the movements, and at the free moment, dove in.

Water and toxins swirled around him. Massive vines missed him by inches as he swam toward Soaf-ie. Muscles screamed, and his head throbbed. As he reached her, a vine came crashing through the water towards them. He turned just in time and fired his phaser. Not sure if it would have an effect, he was grateful to see it slice through the organism with deadly force. The water around Geordi suddenly filled with massive waves of sound that could only be described as pain… endless pain.

Geordi grabbed onto Soaf-ie and turned the phaser to the near wall – the other side of which was… space. He aimed the phaser at its highest setting and fired.

Instantly, Geordi and Soaf-ie were sucked into the blackness of space, missing the automatic force field safety by milliseconds. Geordi could feel the air pulled from his lungs with wrenching violence. He tapped his communicator, hoping the water hadn't damaged it, and grateful when his body dematerialized, and transported away…

…To Transporter Room 3. Geordi punched his communicator. "La Forge to Yar. Tasha, hit the radiation now!"

Geordi waited for what seemed like an age, and then –

"The plants are… shrinking. Force field holding. Seems you were right." Geordi collapsed with a gasp of relief.

Geordi stood before Captain Picard in his ready room. Neither he nor Lieutenant Soaf-ie needed much time in Sickbay, and repairs to the hull were underway.

"Sir, I tender my resig—"

"As you damn well should, Lieutenant." Picard's voice boomed around the room like a boxer hitting a practice pad. His body heat high, and pulse elevated. Angry, in other words.

"We do not go in guns blazing, we do not threaten lifeforms because it is convenient, and we do not wildly experiment because it's quicker. Patience and thoughtfulness, Lieutenant. If we don't have that, people get hurt, most of all… us." Picard let out a sigh. "And Starfleet does not ruin a life, because of a single accident. No one was hurt, and thankfully the bulkhead can be repaired."

"Sir, I… almost killed someone."

"Yes, you did. Learn from that mistake, and pass on that lesson to others, so we all may be better for it. Do you understand?" Geordi considered, then straightened.

"Yes, sir. What will happen to Ruan IV, sir?"

"For the moment, nothing. They now view us as heretics, and cut off communications." Geordi lowered his head. "In time, Lieutenant, as with all things, we may find a common ground again."

"Yes, sir." Geordi turned to leave. As the door opened, he stared at his station on the bridge.

"Captain? My training was in engineering. With your permission, I'd like to revisit that, with the aim of transferring away from tactical. Off-hours, of course. I think maybe my place is solving problems, rather than identifying them."

Picard let out a small smile. While many more discussions were needed, Geordi had a feeling his journey on this *Enterprise* was only just beginning… ✦

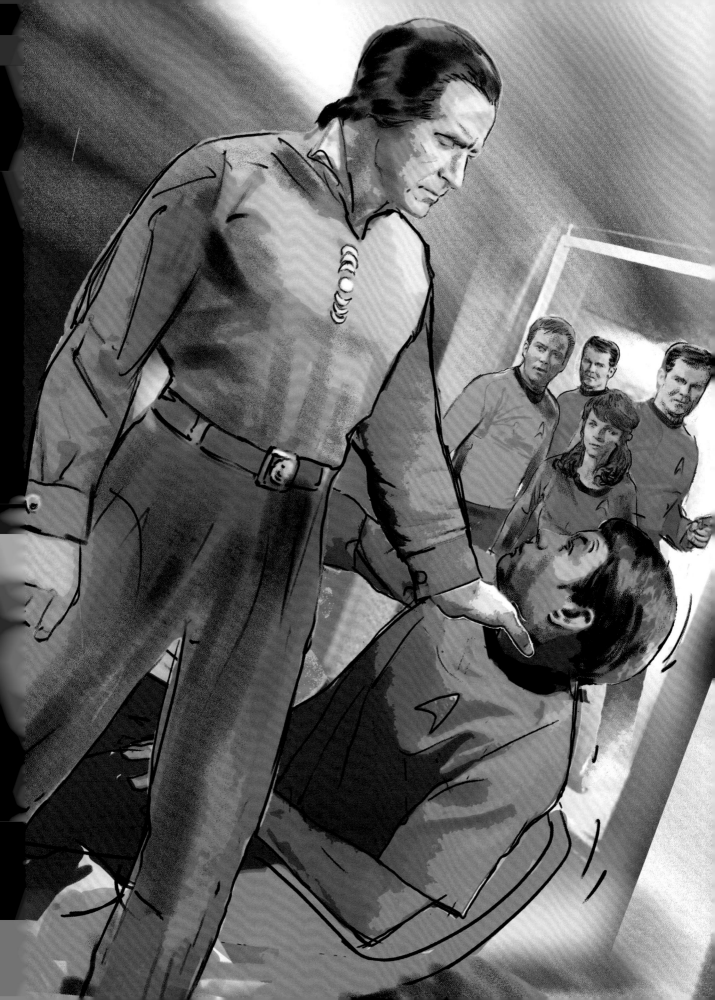

EXPLORE THE
STAR TREK COLLECTION!

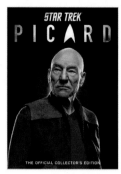

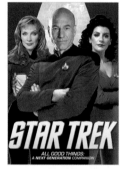